I hope you enjoy!

~AJCooper

Wicked Dreams

by

Amy J. Cooper

authorHOUSE™

1663 Liberty Drive, Suite 200
Bloomington, Indiana 47403
(800) 839-8640
www.AuthorHouse.com

This book is a work of fiction. People, places, events, and situations are the product of the author's imagination. Any resemblence to actual persons, living or dead, or historical events, is purely coincidental.

© 2005 Amy J. Cooper. All Rights Reserved.

No part of this book may be reproduced, stored in a retrieval system, or transmitted by any means without the written permission of the author.

First published by AuthorHouse 03/07/05

> ISBN: 1-4208-1983-6 (e)
> ISBN: 1-4208-1982-8 (sc)

Library of Congress Control Number: 2005902127

Printed in the United States of America
Bloomington, Indiana

This book is printed on acid-free paper.

For Emily

(August 27, 1989 – June 6, 2000)
-By Her Companion, Amy J. Cooper

Although you walked on all fours,
    covered with the softest of fur,
        although you were these,
               you were more human,
                   than most I've known.

With an adoring love,
    And a spirit that danced in the sun,
        swayed with the moon,
           filled my heart,
                filled my soul.

I cannot bear that your soft, warm body is gone.
    I can only feel peace that you
        have no pain,
           that you wait for me,

And that your warm and loving spirit,
    will embrace me until I am with you again.

I must accept your new form,
    and know that all the pain I must endure,
        is yet a small price,
           for the gift of you.

God Bless Dr. Burns and all our friends at Red Maples
Their love and kindness is truly a gift.

"... something wicked this way comes..."
-William Shakespeare (1564-1616)

Chapter 1

It was getting much harder to see. They were losing the light. But soon their eyes would adjust to the darkness of night, although it might be better if they weren't able to see it. He did not know yet what it looked like. He only knew that it was evil. He could feel his legs becoming hard. The muscles were stiffening. The two had been running for a long time now, a long time without rest, food or water.

He looked down at her, his companion, as she was running beside him. She had been by his side since that first day they met. He couldn't remember how long ago he had broken away from the rest of his people. He remembered, though, that he had journeyed alone through the wilderness for many births of the new moon. He'd been alone, but not lonely. He never desired companionship until she came along.

And then he became sick. He didn't know if it was from some strange new food he had found in unfamiliar woods or from one of the many bites and scratches that were the price he paid for a good hunt. The sickness quickly became worse. He fell in and out of consciousness for several days with a fiery fever. And then she came to him from some unknown place. She hunted for him and fed him. She curled up next to him and kept him warm as he slept. For though he was burning with fever, he was chilled. She saved his life, this stranger. And ever since, they had hunted side by side, roamed side by side and slept side by side. The respect, love and understanding they had for each other had grown so deep they had become as one.

He glanced quickly down at her again. He could tell by her breathing she was not going to be able to run much longer, and he knew he couldn't run without her. He knew she was the reason he'd found the strength to run this far. He could see beads of blood splattered across her face. He also felt the pain in his face. It came from the branches and vines that had been cutting through their skin since they had begun this long run. Her stride had lost its grace as her bloodied feet forced her to run with a limp. He saw the pain and the fear in her eyes, and he knew when she looked up at him, she was seeing the same in his own.

And then, in the same instant, their thoughts being one, they stopped. Together they turned to face what would be coming soon. Breathing was painful for both of them. Their lungs had been deprived of good air for too long. The sun was gone now and the moon danced in shadows across her face as he stood looking at her. He loved her so deeply that he couldn't remember when it began. He only knew that it would never end. Not even today, the day they would die. She looked up at him and he knew that she felt the same. Together they were about to fight their last battle. And he knew that in all of his years of warring, he'd known no warrior that he would rather have by his side.

They listened. He knew her ears were much more sensitive than his so he relied on her, watching her for any sign of sound. There was a slight breeze that made the vines on the trees and the smaller branches sway in the moonlight. Their dance was eerie and he felt chills down his spine. But other than the dances of the vines, there was no sound. She tilted her head up, and with her nose in the air, she drew in quick little breaths. Again, this sense was stronger than his. He watched her intently as she investigated the breeze for any hint of the foul air that came with the evil one. Again, nothing.

Perhaps it was only for an hour, but they stood together that way for what seemed like an eternity. They knew it was out there. And they knew it was waiting and watching. It knew to stay just so far away so that she wouldn't be able to pick up a sound or scent from it. It was waiting for them to rest. It knew that they must be caught by surprise. That would be the only way.

They had never known anything like this. They had never seen evil before. When they had shared blood together, it was only for the pure hunt of food for nourishment, for survival. They only took what they needed and they used every part of what they took. They thanked their higher power every night at the fire for what they had been given and they always gave respect to their mother earth. All creatures in these woods were like that. Nothing was evil. Nothing, that is, until now.

And they stood, this wild male and this beautiful and wild female. They stood together as one. And they waited. Suddenly, her body tensed and she flashed a look at him. He knew. They looked at each other and their eyes spoke with honor that they would fight 'til death, neither leaving the other's side.

Yes, now he could smell it too. It was the smell of evil. It was the smell of horrible deaths and sicknesses and pain and suffering. It was the smell of useless deaths, deaths simply for the sake of death and not for the purpose of food for survival. Although they had never known evil before, they somehow both understood that this was it in its purest form. And they stood ready.

It sprang suddenly from the darkness. It went for her first because it knew that although she was smaller, she was quick and could only be conquered by surprise. She gave out a yelp, half from surprise, half from pain. She fought and writhed under the pressure of its weight. Her teeth were bloody and there were torn fragments of its fur on her face and in her mouth. The horrible taste made her fight even harder. The man was beating it with a large limb from a nearby oak. His unexpected strength came from some deep unknown place in his soul. He knew he would protect his companion with everything he had.

The beast turned to face him, ignoring the bloody, but not beaten, female. It was confused. It did not understand why the man had not fled in fear. Why was he protecting his companion? It hesitated in its confusion and the female took advantage of this fleeting moment and leaped at the back of the beast's neck. She tried to get a good hold and was able to do some damage, but not enough to stop the beast from grabbing her from his back and throwing her hard against the ground. Again, she yelped. She was dazed from the throw and shook her head trying to get her vision to clear. When she did, she saw the beast beating the man with that same bloody tree limb,

Wicked Dreams

which moments ago had been the weaponry held by him. The man was trying to fight back, but it was more an effort to protect his body from the hard and bloody blows.

The female knew that she had only an instant left to fight back. She knew that the man would die any second if she didn't kill the beast now. She let out a low, blood curdling growl which made the beast turn to face her. It didn't understand why she was still there. Again, the female used the beast's moment of perplexity to prevail in the battle. She lunged at it with her mouth wide open. In the moonlight, the beast could see the glimmer of her long sharp teeth just as she landed on it. She tore into its throat, tore for that spot her senses told her the beast had. That Achilles on the neck wherefrom the juice of the evil thing's life could be drained. The beast let out a hissing gurgle as it fell to the ground, its neck spurting the stench, the dark fluid of its being. The female hobbled over to where the man lay and curled by his side. They shivered together as they watched the beast turn into a deep gray smoke and fade away into the cool and gentle night.

They were too weak from battle to find another place to sleep. Together they found some wood and built a fire to keep the chill of the night away. He cleaned her wounds as best he could and packed them with medicinal leaves and mud. He felt relief because he could see that although her wounds were deep and painful, they would heal in time. When he was finished taking care of her, she turned to him and licked his wounds clean and cuddled against him near the fire. They would keep each other warm and would survive the night. For they had survived the fight, the good fight. And they had fought as one. And they would continue their days as one. This beautiful and good wild man and this beautiful and good wild dog.

They dreamed as they always dreamed that night. She in his dreams, he in hers. They dreamed of the beast and knew they were safe from it. They would be safe in their lifetime, but they feared for the future for they knew that one day it would be back. For evil is an army of manifestations and scattered through time it sends a scout forward just like this one. Its duty is clearly defined. It must seek out a soldier from the other side, the side of good. It peers into the soul of this enemy to determine its strength. If the enemy is undefeatable and with companion, the scout will sink back into the shadow of darkness and wait until commanded to slither out again. The man and the bitch knew that their descendants would join for battle, would join for the good fight once again. They dreamed of this battle and feared for the future. He groaned in his sleep, she growled, and together they dreamed the wicked dream.

"... an' the Gobble-uns 'at gits you ef you don't watch out!"

James Whitcomb Riley (1849 - 1916)

Chapter 2

It was 1975. She was 13. An unlucky number for an unlucky young lady in an unlucky life. She was miserable. But she had her dog, Molly, to get her through. And that was what she did. She just got through, somehow. Molly was a "mutt." Dianna never understood why people would say that and laugh or just stand there with a smirk. Like being a mutt was supposed to be an insult. Dianna knew that it was something special for a dog to be a pure breed, but she felt that it was something extra special to be a "blend," as she preferred to call it. And Molly was a beautiful blend. Her warm, soft fur was splattered with shades of brown, white and black. Her face was mostly brown and white, and her back was a big splotch of dark brown that faded into black. Her legs looked like a deer to Dianna. They were a light, tan brown with smatterings of white. And Molly had the biggest, warmest brown eyes that Dianna could ever imagine.

Dianna loved Molly and they went for walks every day after school. She hated to use the collar and leash, but her mother insisted. And Dianna knew in her heart that if Molly should run free, she could get lost and that some mean person would probably find her and hurt her. Dianna tried to explain to her mother that if

Molly would just be allowed to go out on her own a little at a time, eventually she would walk comfortably alongside Dianna without that stupid leash. She knew in time Molly could learn their new neighborhood and could learn to look both ways before she crossed the street. But as usual, her mother didn't have time to argue. She only had time to set the rules and then go out to some bar or other and get drunk.

So here they were on this cool autumn evening, a skinny little freckled girl and her mutt. Dianna talked to Molly on their walks. She told Molly everything. She believed that dogs understood, and she could tell by those big brown eyes looking up at her, that Molly felt Dianna's pain. Dianna's mother and father had recently divorced. It had all happened so fast. All of a sudden, her father didn't come home anymore at night. And then her mother was packing boxes to move Dianna and her sister to another city. Other than not getting to see her father every day, Dianna's life hadn't changed much. Sure the school was different, but Dianna never had any trouble making friends. She was a loner for the most part, but people seemed to feel comfortable with her. She filled her time studying hard, always searching for a perfection that only she would know. And she had Molly.

They walked on down the sidewalk exchanging glances while engaged in what would seem to be a one-sided conversation to those who would pass by. She was oblivious to the drawn curtains of her neighbors' houses as they were carefully pulled aside a few inches for a better peek at the strange, quiet girl who talked to her dog. Even if Dianna had seen them, it wouldn't have made a difference. She loved her Molly.

They were approaching the sound of yapping dogs. Dianna hated that house. The people who lived in that house were dirty and their small yard was one giant mud puddle. They had about ten dogs in the yard, each one tied to a tree or a pipe stuck in the ground. It broke Dianna's heart to see those poor animals treated that way.

"Don't they get it, Molly? We're all the same. Those people wouldn't like to be treated like that."

Molly looked up at Dianna with her soft eyes, which seemed to say she understood. She knew that Dianna had been going around the neighborhood getting quite a few of her neighbors to call in to report these mean people. And it finally looked as though all of that hard work would pay off. Rumor had it that the day after tomorrow the dogs would be taken away. Dianna dreaded deeply the thought that some of these animals would be put to sleep. She could only comfort herself with the thought that at least the dogs would be happier in heaven free from the suffering they had endured here on earth.

Suddenly, Dianna felt Molly tense. Molly stood rigid and let out a low growl such that Dianna had never heard from her before. Before she knew what was happening, a dog twice the size of Molly was sprinting toward them, baring sharp teeth from his foaming mouth. He let out a hideous growl that sent shivers down Dianna's spine. He smelled like something so awful that it made Dianna's stomach instantly cramp and she found herself gagging. That smell wasn't the smell of a plain old dirty dog. It wasn't the smell of anything Dianna could remember having smelled before. But she was lying to herself. She did know. She knew it was the smell of something bad and she knew that it wanted her Molly.

Molly left Dianna's side and stood in front of her. She knew the animal was evil and she would not let it touch her Dianna. Suddenly, the animal lunged for Molly and began biting at her. The leash became entwined around Molly's legs as she tried to circle around the animal to keep it away from Dianna. Dianna couldn't bear the sound of snapping teeth and the blood she saw on Molly's back. Before she even knew what she was doing, she flung herself at Molly and wrapped her body around the dog to protect her. There was a pause in the attack as the raging animal appeared confused by this act. Then it began to attack Dianna, biting up and down her bare arms. Dianna felt the pain and she saw the blood, but all she could do was hold Molly even tighter.

Just as Dianna thought that this was how her life would end, she heard the sound of a honking horn. She carefully pulled her head ever so slightly out from under her tucked position to see a school bus pull up with the driver honking the horn over and over in short warning blasts. He stopped the bus and came crashing through its doors with a baseball bat in his hand, screaming at the attacking dog. The animal fled in fear and the bus driver and Dianna watched as it seemed to evaporate in the dusk.

After being assured that Dianna and Molly didn't live far, the bus driver watched as the two limped down the sidewalk. He kept a watchful eye out for the mad dog. He waited there as the sun was setting and the air was cooling; he waited until he could see the two little warriors no more.

Dianna and Molly had survived the attack, and after some antiseptic, stitches, bandages, antibiotics and a series of unpleasant shots, they were both back to normal. The people in the neighborhood said the dog had come from that dirty yard, but Dianna and Molly knew differently. That had been no ordinary dog. In fact, as time went by, Dianna couldn't quite convince herself that it had, in fact, even been a dog. The one thing that remained vivid in her memory was the smell. That smell belonged to something bad, some unknown evil, and it would remain ever so repugnant in her memory for the rest of her life. And for the rest of her life, Dianna would feel a kinship to all animals, and especially to dogs. As Dianna continued on the road of "growing up" so would grow the mutual respect between her and all of the furry four-legged creatures she would come to know.

"...to fetch her poor dog a bone..."

- Old Mother Hubbard

Chapter 3

She had finally gone and done it. Yep. And it felt oh, so good. Dianna lay quietly in the bath, which was pouring over with bubbles the scent of hyacinth. This definitely felt good. She had taken the day off from work. Here it was mid-afternoon on a wonderfully clear and cool spring weekday and she was soaking in the bath tub. Ahhh, what a life. She heard a soft and comforting moan as she looked over the edge of the tub in time to see Emily stretch out and give a yawn.

"Feels good, doesn't it, babe?"

Emily answered with a quick wag of her tail and a sleepy glance up to Dianna. They had worn each other out that morning running through the woods and playing with Emily's blue rubber ball. Emily never quite seemed to catch on to the concept of catching the ball and bringing it back to Dianna. She would never let go of it. With a mockery of growling and snarling, she would hold on to it with her teeth and soon the twosome would become intertwined in some rough and tumble game that made onlookers question the sanity of both. One of Dianna's friends had once said that Emily didn't know how to let go of the ball because she was a stupid dog. Unfortunately the fate of the Dalmatian is to have a reputation of ignorance. Dianna knew better. She knew that in Emily's mind this was the way that the game was supposed to be played. That retrieving stuff was for the birds. This was supposed to be a contact sport.

Dianna felt herself drifting off to sleep in the warmth of her bath. And as she faded into dreamland, her thoughts turned to romance. Not that she had been having any; just that she thought it might be nice to try again. What ever did happen to Paul?

Dianna's mind went back to the day she had met Paul. It was a cold and dreary day in December. But the weather never seemed to keep Dianna and Emily inside. They had been romping in the park. And as always, in no time at all, they were both caked in mud. It had been snowing and sleeting followed by several days of warmth, just enough for the ground to begin to thaw. Perfect conditions for Emily and Dianna to mud romp. They had just worn each other out when Dianna realized that they were not alone. Sitting on a bench about one hundred yards away sat a tall, lean man. From where she stood, Dianna thought he looked handsome, which to her meant that he was either the kind and handsome type, who of course would thus be married; or he was the cruel and handsome type, which then would mean that he was available. She had been burned too many times to really care, though. It was just an assumption based on curiosity.

As she was toweling the mud off Emily so they could get into the car, she noticed the stranger walking by. Yes, he was tall. And, yes, he was handsome. Dianna didn't want to know anything else. The beating of her heart was enough to tell her to "get the hell out of Dodge." She climbed into her car and decided right then that she would not give the handsome stranger another moment's thought.

Amy J. Cooper

Several weeks later, Dianna found herself at a wine and cheese doing at a small, local art gallery. She loved art. She had never studied it, but loved it all the same. She was looking over a brooding impressionism of a wintry sunset when she felt someone standing near. She looked up into his face wondering where she had seen him before. His deep, grey eyes were gazing down into hers.

"Do you like pasta?" the handsome stranger asked.

"What in the ..... Huh? Err, I mean, yes, I do." *Where in the heck did that come from?* Dianna wondered to herself.

"Uh, I mean, would you like to have dinner with me?" He thought he'd try again.

"Umm. I'm not sure." *Who is this guy?* Dianna continued to wonder. Then suddenly it came to her. *Oh, I know! He's the guy from the park!*

After mulling it over for a moment or two, Dianna realized that she didn't feel afraid. Even though she thought that it was odd that this stranger who she had first seen at the park a few weeks ago should turn up here at the gallery to ask her out, she felt that it would be all right.

And it was all right. They ate spaghetti together like they were old pals, splashing tomato sauce over their chins as they puckered their cheeks and sucked up the long delicious noodles. It had been awhile since Dianna had been on a date, but she didn't remember ever feeling so comfortable on a first one. They sat for hours after dinner sharing wine and stories and favorites of music and books.

Dianna loved everything about Paul. He had an incredibly warped sense of humor, he was a great thinker, he was sensitive and kind and generous, and he was passionate. He seemed to feel the same way about her. This was even harder for Dianna to grasp. She had never been in a relationship before where she was accepted for just being herself. It felt so strange to be with a man who accepted her for all of her decisions, all of her faults, and all of her thoughts.

"What ever did happen to Paul?" Dianna asked Emily as she stepped out of the tub, awkwardly balancing herself as she tried to find footing around the resting dog. As she began to dry herself, Dianna thought more about Paul. He had just sort of vanished into thin air. It had been, what, maybe three months since she had seen him. No, it was more than that. Here it was June and she hadn't seen him since January. *My, how time flies.*

Dianna's thoughts were taken away from her when Emily began to bark. She was stretched out on the bathroom rug and all four feet were in motion. She was baring her teeth and emitting a low and lonely growl. After a few seconds of desperate growling, she let out another muffled bark.

"Hey, Girl, are you chasing after the boogie man?"

Emily continued to growl and run in her sleep.

"Hey, Girl, wake up." Dianna gently rubbed on Emily's pink belly.

Emily didn't respond.

Dianna began to shake Emily, at first softly, but then more aggressively. "Wake up, Emily! Wake up, now!" She had to shake the dog for a full minute, but then Emily finally looked up at Dianna with glazed eyes. Those strange eyes seemed to look right through Dianna, but then they moved slowly as though they were following some invisible being as it floated through the room and out the door. Then Emily looked up at Dianna with eyes that seemed to show sadness and fear at the same time.

"What was it, Girl?"

Emily's eyes slowly returned to their normal intense blue and she began to wag her tail.

"Oh, you're such a good girl, Emily. Let's go get you a bone."

Emily jumped up, stretched her front legs and then her hind legs, and happily followed Dianna to the kitchen. She knew these bones weren't real bones. They were some kind of man-made treat, but she didn't care. They tasted pretty good. And she knew that Dianna was rewarding her. She believed Dianna didn't quite understand why she was rewarding her, but soon she would help Dianna to understand the good fight. Soon she would have to show her the truth of her wicked dreams. Soon. She wasn't sure exactly when, but she knew that somehow she would know when the time was right.

In the meantime, she would enjoy her "bone."

"Youth will be served, every dog has his day, and mine has been a fine one."

- *George Borrow (1803-1881)*

Chapter 4

It was a wonderfully warm and sunny August day. Dianna couldn't believe her luck. Today was the day she had been planning for, when some of her friends would come over for a cookout. Her thoughts drifted to Paul, wondering where he was and what he was doing that day. Dianna was sure he had long since forgotten about her, but she wasn't quite able to put all thoughts of him out of her mind. There was something about him. She hoped something would happen soon to help her forget. These thoughts filled her mind as she put the finishing touch, a dash of paprika, on her deviled eggs.

Dianna could hear Emily in the other room making her muffled "woof" sounds. It seemed that lately Emily was doing that more and more. What could she be dreaming? The sounds were getting louder and were beginning to take on a note of urgency. Dianna couldn't stand it any longer and she quickly stepped out of the kitchen and into her living room. Emily was there sleeping on the couch with all four legs in running motion. She was baring her teeth and there was that low and lonely growl again.

"Emily, wake up!" Dianna gently shook Emily. "Wake up, Baby! Wake up!"

But Emily didn't wake up. She kept on dreaming, running and growling in whatever dreamscapes she had found.

"Emily, you're scaring me! Wake up! Wake up!"

And just as Dianna reached panic, Emily awoke. And just like the other times, it seemed to take a moment for her eyes to come into focus. Those few moments, as always, were the strangest to Dianna. Those moments brought a chill down her spine; those moments when Emily's eyes would follow some invisible being as it seemed to float through the room and then down the hallway. Then Emily looked up into Dianna's eyes. She seemed a little frightened and also, as before, a little sad. Then her tail began to wiggle a little, increasing in tempo until it was in a full scale wag as she gave her master's hand a gentle lick.

"Are you loving on that dog again?" came a soft voice from the living room doorway.

Dianna turned to see her best friend and next-door neighbor, Jennifer Caldwell. She was a beautiful woman, the same age as Dianna, 36. She wasn't really taller than Dianna, but her long legs and thin figure made her seem much taller. They had become great friends when Dianna first moved into this house five years ago following her divorce. Jennifer was also a divorcee, but she kept most of her past life private. In fact, the few things that she had told Dianna were the only confidences she had shared with anyone since she had moved to Columbus, Ohio six years earlier.

"Yeah, I'm loving on her. She was having another one of her nightmares. This is starting to really spook me," Dianna answered as she rubbed her hands

Wicked Dreams

vigorously up and down her arms trying to shake off the sudden chill she felt.

"Dogs dream, Honey. You know that."

"I know, but not like this. This is something more."

Emily stretched out, reaching out with all four legs as if everything were just fine on this warm and sunny day. Jennifer and Dianna had no idea the dog could understand everything they were saying and knew Dianna was much closer to the truth now. Emily could feel the time approaching. Soon. It would be soon.

Before anything further could be said, there was the sound of a car horn coming up the driveway. It was Lucy and Dave. Dianna had been friends with Dave since high school. They had always chummed around together, through college and ever since.

It was Dianna who brought Lucy and Dave together during college. There was a quaint coffee house just on the outskirts of campus that Dianna and Dave would frequent. A small stage towards the front of the little shop oftentimes played host to a struggling writer who would unveil his soul to the audience, seeking criticism but wanting none. Dianna had come alone that night and had finally brought some of her poetry to read. She was sitting at a small table in the corner shuffling through the papers and struggling with the decision to come forward and read when she heard a whispered voice next to her.

"Go for it."

"I don't think I can. Wait, that's not right. I don't think I want to."

"I know. Me too."

Dianna turned to see a dark-haired, dark skinned beautiful woman. She appeared so exotic that Dianna couldn't accept that those common words, "Go for it," could have come from those lips.

"Name is Lucy. What's yours?"

"Dianna."

And that was that. The two became fast friends while Dave was out of town visiting his folks. And when he returned two weeks later, Dianna saw to it that he met Lucy. She knew they would be a perfect match. And they were.

That seems like it was only yesterday, Dianna thought to herself. But before she could give it any further thought, more friends and neighbors began to arrive. Soon the grill was smoking and the air was filled with the wonderful aroma of hamburgers and veggie burgers cooking. The sounds of peaceful music drifted through the wooded yard from Dianna's stereo, which had been brought out to the patio for the party.

*"... with mash and antique pageantry,
Such sights as youthful poets dream,
On summer eves by haunted stream."*

- John Milton (1608-1674)

Chapter 5

Paul didn't know where the dog had come from. He wasn't even really sure how long it had been hanging around. At first, he would just sit out on his back deck and talk to it. Slowly, the dog became more and more comfortable with the man's voice and would creep a little closer to the wooden deck. He liked the smell of the wood. The houses around here were few and far between, but they all had these wooden decks in the back. He had seen the humans who lived in the houses sitting day after day on chairs with soft cushions on those decks, watching the water. He understood the allure of the water. He could understand things more clearly when he stared into the waves. And he found that this deck was best suited for water thinking than those others. It didn't have that shiny look and it smelled like real wood. There were spots that stayed damp for a long time after a rain. He liked that the man left it be. He liked the way the man let the garden on the front of the house grow wild too. The smells were good smells from that garden. And the butterflies were many here. That was a good sign. Yes, the dog was almost certain that this was where he would begin to prepare for the good fight. And this was the man, the man who would help him.

Eventually, the man began to bring warm dinners out onto the deck - two plates. It was the beginning of fall and the warm food took the chill off. The dog would eat hungrily and then settle at the man's feet and fall into a peaceful slumber to the smooth sounds of the man's voice. Sometimes he would dream. It must have scared the man because the dog would wake up with the man on his knees before him. He would be cuddling the dog and soothing him. When the dog would adjust to reality, blink his eyes and lick the man on his face, he always noticed the tension leave the man's body. Oh, yes, this was the right man. This man was one of those few, the few who truly cared. This one had already begun to fight the good fight, even though it had been many years ago and lost in the man's memory. But he would remember. Soon.

"Dog and Butterfly"
          -The Wilson Sisters

Chapter 6

She was warm and comfortable stretched out on her comforter. The dream started as it always did, soft and warm. She was slowly floating toward a small field of flowers. So many scents. And the butterflies. Beautiful dancing wings fluttered about the multi-colored petals; dancing, dancing, all in a sort of rhythmic time. She felt good. It was good.

Suddenly, the butterflies floated over her head. They formed a ring that spun around and around her head, faster and faster. And just as suddenly as the dance had begun, it stopped. The butterflies hesitated for a moment, hovering over Emily's head and then they were gone. They seemed to vanish in the breeze that Emily hadn't sensed until now.

The wind. It carried that smell. That bad smell. The evil thing was near. The warmth of the sun was gone. It had been extinguished by the clouds and the cold air, the bad air. It was here. Suddenly Emily was desperately seeking the strength to keep from vomiting. That smell. That evil smell. She made herself fill her mind with the memory of the colors, the scents, the dance of the butterflies. Then she was filled with the courage to stand strong and to fight the good fight. She had done it in many dreams before. But was this really a dream? No, Emily had learned after the first few battles that this was more than just a dream. This was the reality that was normally not seen, the reality that hides each day in the shadows of the sun, the reality that it is often felt but seldom seen. This reality can only be seen by very few, those few who truly care.

But this battle was going to be different. *But what made it different?* She was not alone, and yet she could see no other presence. She tilted her head into the cold breeze and tried to read the wind. She picked up a faint scent that reminded her of cold winter days when she would lay snuggled on the rug on the kitchen floor. Her master would be making something sweet in the oven and the smell of it cooking would interweave with her master's song, something she hummed. All warm and cozy while the winter air froze outside, that's how Emily felt now. She knew with all of her heart that this new smell was a good smell, and that this unseen presence was a good presence.

"The trouble with our times is that the future is not what it used to be"

-Paul Valery (1871-1945)

Chapter 7

Even though only a little over a month had passed since the relationship had begun, the effect it had on him was great. There were no more tangles or burrs or weeds in his long golden hair. He had a spry step as he moved along the beach. His ribs were no longer jutting out from his lean body. His large brown eyes glowed.

At this moment, he was laying on the rug in front of the warm fire listening to the man's voice. The man was speaking to him so carefully. He seemed to have a difficult time finding the right words. He didn't realize that it didn't matter. The dog would take his understanding from so much more than just the words. There were the thoughts that hung in the air over them. There was the look on the man's face and the tone of his voice. The dog knew. He knew it was getting close. Soon he would have to let the man see. Soon the good fight would come.

In his visions, in his dreams, the dog had recently come to a new realization, one that gave him comfort. They would not be alone. There were two more who would be joining them as leaders in the war. Two more. The vision was still too new, still too vague to know if they were of canine or of human descent. And there

Amy J. Cooper

was more. He felt that these two were close, very close, and that soon others would follow. There would be more. Although he found comfort in knowing that many would be joining them, he felt anxious that the Great Spirit felt that so many were needed. This would be the battle of good versus evil, and there would be fire, blood and the loss of life.

*"...The days may come, the days may go,
But still the hands of memory weave
The blissful dreams of long ago."*

-George Cooper (1838-1927)

Chapter 8

It was so wonderfully sunny and warm without a cloud in the sky. And oh, did it ever feel good. The place looked familiar, and yet as though it was from some dream. Sam was with him. Yes, Sam. For some reason, it wasn't until just this moment that he knew the dog's name. Sam. The dog looked up into his eyes right at that moment, as though he heard his name spoken. His golden hair reflected the rays of the sun as he seemed to dance over the wild flowers and weeds. They were going somewhere and it was important that they get there soon. If only Paul knew where that somewhere was. But he did. Or did he? It was somewhere in the back of his mind, just enough out of reach that he couldn't quite grasp it. He would learn later that there was a reason for that. For if he had indeed had a vivid picture of where the two were headed, he would have surely turned around and run as far and as fast as his legs could carry him.

This place they were going to, it seemed to already be sucking strength from him. He felt weary, but not alone. It wasn't just the companionship of his newfound four-legged friend that he drew comfort from. There was somebody else. He wasn't sure who, though. It was nagging at the back of his mind, but he couldn't quite put his finger on it. It was someone he knew. It was someone he had met. It was a female. And she was not alone. She was with a companion. *Was her companion on four legs too?*

He suddenly realized that their pace had slowed. Sam was hunkered down and was showing his teeth. He let out a low growl that was enveloped by the sound of the wind coming through the field and through the trees of the nearby woods. He didn't seem frightened. In fact, Paul thought it odd that the animal actually seemed brave and ready to do battle. Battle? *Battle with who..... or was it battle with what?* Paul didn't know. He was just beginning to let himself laugh this all off as some kind of sick joke when he sensed it, when he smelled it.

At first the odor was faint. Then the clouds that had been invisible until now were suddenly everywhere. They came in with the cold wind that was now singing louder and louder amongst the weeds and wildflowers. The song was coming from the branches of the trees in the nearby woods. It was getting louder and louder until the sound was not a song anymore. It was becoming a scream.

Paul realized that he was covering his ears with his hands, trying to block out the hideous noise. The dog stood poised with his nose in the air. He was picking up something.

"What is it, boy? What's out there?"

But Sam remained erect. A statue standing guard. *Guard against what?*

Wicked Dreams

As the wind grew sharper, it brought the smell closer to the pair. The smell. *What was that?* It grew stronger and stronger.

Although Paul had never smelled that smell before, somehow he knew what it was. It was bad. It was evil. *This must be what hell smells like.* Sam knew. He was still letting out that low and eerie growl. And yet, he remained unmoved. Solid. Still. Waiting.

The smell grew stronger. It was making Paul feel nauseous. It was horrible. It was worse than horrible. *It was..... it was..... Oh, Gawd!* It was unimaginable, and yet familiar.

"Yea, though I walk through the shadow of death, I will fear no evil..."

It was a real smell. It was something he had tried to forget. It was.. it was....

Suddenly, Paul's mind flashed back to when he was 13 years old. He had a paper route then. Brownsville was a small sleepy town with only an evening paper. Paul would ride his bike along and toss the papers up onto the porches of the old homes of his neighbors. Some of the folks were stiff with old age. And for those special clients, Paul would park his bike and go up and ring the doorbell, saving his customers from unnecessary stooping to pick up a paper. He loved doing it, and they loved him because he cared.

But this one night something was wrong. It was one of those evenings in early autumn when the air was crisp and clear. The sun had already begun to sink in the western sky. Unaccustomed to the early darkness that fell about him, Paul found himself just a bit spooked as he pedaled along delivering the local news. At first there was just the faintest scent of smoke. Someone was already using their fireplace. What a cozy feeling this brought to Paul as he lifted his nose into the air, just as he had seen his dog do, to take in the full aroma of the night air. Soon, though, the smell became less comforting. Something was wrong. It was too strong. It wasn't the smell of firewood. It was more. It was bad. And it was just around the corner.

When Paul turned that corner, he saw the Miller house ablaze. Old neighbors were beginning to come out in their tired, faded flannel robes and slippers to see what was going on. But there was no Mr. Miller and no Scout, his dog. Where were they?

Paul had never been close to a real fire before, but he was suddenly filled with such a deep fear it was as though he knew exactly what it was like to be in one. He knew he did not want to go any closer to the flames. But where were Mr. Miller and Scout? Paul knew they were home. He had stopped by what seemed like just moments ago to deliver their paper. He had petted Scout while discussing sports scores with Mr. Miller.

Suddenly it was as though hands were pushing on Paul's shoulders pushing him closer and closer to the burning house. *I don't want to go in there! I don't want to go!* The invisible hands were patting him on the back as though to comfort him, to let him know that all would be okay. *Okay? How can this be okay?*

There was a fluttering movement in Paul's peripheral vision. And then another one. He couldn't help but to turn his head toward the motion and was surprised to see a cluster of butterflies floating in circles near his head. He recognized some of them from his biology class at school. The dancing wings were from monarch's, tiger swallowtails, zebras and, yes, there was even a great purple hairstreak, Paul's favorite. His mind jumped to thoughts of that butterfly. *Why was it his favorite?* Was it the beautiful, colorful wings, or was it perhaps just the name, as Paul's mother had suggested. But they were there and that was all that mattered. *Why?* Because somehow as they danced about Paul's head, they seemed to be filling his body and mind with strength. It filled him with more than just strength. It filled him with the need, the urgent desire to go into the house. He needed to rescue the old man and his dog. They weren't supposed to die this way. Not by the acts of ... *of what?* There was no time to try to figure it out now.

Before any of the spectators had a chance to seize Paul and stop him, he was running up the front steps, across the porch and into the front door. The house was full of thick smoke and the flames were growing fast as though in any moment the whole place would explode.

Somehow, Paul knew exactly where to go. Later, he would find this somewhat strange since he had never been anywhere but in the front living room of this old house before. He fought his way through the smoke to the kitchen, which was in the back of the house. There on the floor near the back door he could see what looked like someone hunched over. It was too hard to see. *Who was there?* Someone was sitting upright not making a noise. A small bit of wind from somewhere cleared the smoke for just a moment, just barely long enough that Paul could tell he was looking at two pointed ears standing straight up.

"Scout!"

The answer was a whimper, and probably, hidden in the smoke, a wag of the tail.

"Hey, Boy! Where's the old man?"

Paul moved closer to the whimpering animal, and as he neared Scout, he realized why the dog wouldn't move. Stretched out there on the floor was the old man. His arm was extended as though he had been reaching for the door when he had collapsed with smoke-filled lungs. Scout had his own door cut into the bottom of that back door. He could have escaped the inferno, but there was no way he was going to leave his master.

Paul stooped down and grabbed the old man by his thin shoulders. It was easy to lift him up over his back. Mr. Miller had lost a lot of weight since his wife, Anna, had passed away a few years ago. Paul found a dish towel on the kitchen counter and somehow knew to use it to hold on to the knob of the back door. And he knew he needed to move fast.

"Okay, Scout, when I pull this door open, you run ahead. I'll be right behind you. Okay"

The dog cocked his head and wagged his tail in understanding.

Paul never knew where his strength came from that day. Somehow he had managed to get Scout and Mr. Miller out of the house and into the yard where they both began to recover from the smoke. He didn't know what had given him the courage to go into that burning house.

The authorities never were able to determine what had started the fire. It was a great mystery. What Paul remembered the most about it was that horrible smell. He was never able to understand just what that smell

Wicked Dreams

was. Sure, there were bad smells whenever there was a fire, but this was different. *This was evil.*

Whenever Paul's mind would take him back to that time, he would try to forget the bad smell and only think about the wonderful days that followed the fire. After Mr. Miller was released from the hospital, he was able to restore his home with the insurance money he received. He and Scout became close pals of Paul's. The three of them could often be found wandering through the neighborhood together. On days when Mr. Miller's stiff joints couldn't go for those jaunts, the three would be seen sitting in the rocking chairs on Mr. Miller's front porch, talking and singing and having a good old time.

Many years later, Mr. Miller finally passed on "naturally," as they say. What was comforting to Paul was that when the old man finally died, Scout died the same day. They had grown old together and went to heaven together. Paul found great peace in that thought. The two had been inseparable, and it was comforting to know they would remain together through eternity.

* * * * *

As though waking from a dream, Paul suddenly realized that he and Sam were standing still in the middle of a field. Although the sky was still unusually dark for this time of day, the cloud covering was dissipating and the foul smell that had triggered Paul's childhood memory was only a tinge in the air now. Sam was looking up at Paul. No, he wasn't looking at Paul at all. *What was he looking at?* Paul watched as Sam's eyes moved through the field as though watching something moving away from them. He held his tail out and crooked, his ears were alert, and he was showing his teeth.

"What is it, Boy?"

No response.

"Hey, I'm freaking out here, Sam. What in the hell are you watching?"

The dogs eyes continued to follow the invisible movement until whatever it was seemed to disappear from Sam's vision. Then the dog looked up at Paul and wagged his tail. All was back to normal, whatever that meant...

*"...To sleep, perchance to dream, Aye there's the rub.
For in that sleep of death, what dreams may come..."*

- William Shakespeare (1564-1616)

Chapter 9

Enough days had passed since the "field incident," as Paul referred to it, that he should have been over it. Yet he was still consumed by the thought of it. *What was up with that?* Everything had been fairly peaceful since then. He hadn't even seen Sam have one of his running dreams for several days.

He was sitting on the deck in the old, faded rocker looking out onto the ocean. The waves were dancing in that sort of rhythmic rhyme that could drain all of the worries from your mind and set you to sleeping in a matter of moments. The porch was still old and faded. He probably would never treat the wood. It looked fine to him. He knew that Sam liked it. Ever since the days had become warmer, Sam had been spending most of his time out here sunbathing. He would always sniff around the porch, and then once his investigation was completed, he would turn around in a circle three times, let out a low moan and then settle down for a nap.

Paul was slipping into a warm sunny dream. She was there, that woman. He couldn't quite see her face, but he felt that he knew her. It felt good to be where she was. He had missed her. *Missed who?*

There was Sam. He was sniffing around and wagging his tail.

Where were they? Was this a park? The line of trees looked familiar. He was sure he had been there before.

She was there dancing and laughing. She was camouflaged by a low hanging limb from an old oak tree. In the shadows that played on the grass, he could almost make out her partner, but just barely. *Who was he?* Paul needed to know. It was quickly driving him mad. The jealousy was eating him alive. For one thing, he could tell that the guy was kind of short, not too swift of a dancer either. They were spinning through the shadows until they danced out into the open where the unforgiving light of the sun revealed the woman's mysterious partner. It wasn't a man after all. The partner was female. And what made Paul laugh out loud was that this partner was not even human. She had spots too!

"I'm jealous of a dog!" Paul laughed. Sam was sitting at his feet and wagging his tail.

The two bachelors, side by side, watched as the two familiar females danced and played together. But it was slowly becoming difficult to see them. After a few moments, Paul realized that he was no longer squinting in the sunlight. In fact, he was actually straining his eyes to pick out the two who were across the park lawn.

A flicker off to his left caught Paul's attention. *What was that?* Then there was another one. And then suddenly there was a cluster of butterflies fluttering around his head. The wings were colorful as they glittered in the remaining sunlight. Paul stared at the multiple colors until he picked out the one he was looking for, the great purple hairstreak. *It was here.* In fact, this time there were a few more of them. It gave Paul relief. Well, some relief, but there was also some fear. Paul was grateful for the strength that filled him as the butterflies flew about, but at the same time he was filled with a sense of dread. *This means I need the strength. This means something bad is about to happen.*

Sam was now hunkered down, showing his teeth and emitting that low growl that made Paul shudder. He slowly started to move, one short and deliberate step at a time. He was moving toward the woman and the dog. Paul followed. He didn't know exactly why, but he seemed to be feeling the same pull toward them that Sam was feeling.

As the two moved across the large park, the sky drew darker. And ever so faintly, in the slight breeze that moved through the leaves of the trees, the bad smell was drifting in. Sam lifted his snout into the air and began sniffing. The hair on his back was beginning to stand on end. His growl grew a little more intense.

Slowly they inched toward the spot where the two females had just been dancing and playing. Step by step. Paul still couldn't make them out. The sky had grown so dark and the wind was blowing stronger, bending the limbs of the trees. Visibility was quickly fading. He couldn't quite make them out, but he knew they were there. It wasn't a vision, it wasn't a scent, it was a feeling. *Wait, that's wrong.* Suddenly Paul realized that he could actually smell them. A faint sweet smell floated in the air.

That must be them! But how can I smell that through that other stench? Paul wondered.

There was a crunch in the cluster of trees off to the pair's right. Sam dropped down ready to sprint into attack. Paul stood aghast as he watched something, something he couldn't identify, something that he felt represented all of the evil in the world. That something was slowly crawling out of the woods, slowly moving forward, step by step, closer to where she stood. And then Paul could see her better. *It was her!* It was the woman Paul had seen at the park before. She was here with that spotted dog. *What were they doing?*

"Yeah though I walk through the valley of the shadow of death...." the woman spoke. The dog sat upright next to her. They were facing the black thing. They looked scared but they looked strong. They looked as though they were warriors who had fought side by side many, many times before and were about to set out on another battle, a new one, yet one they seemed familiar with.

"Hey, you!" the woman was now speaking to Paul.

"Me?" He answered, feeling incredibly stupid under the circumstances.

"Yeah, you better let this big guy know real quick what your faith is."

"What my faith is? Well, I was raised as a Congregationalist."

"No! I mean the strength, the strength of your faith in your higher power."

"Well..."

"NOW!"

"I shall fear no evil, for Thou art with me....."

The big dark thing paused. It remained still as though concentrating on the words and reading the strength of them through the scent carried in the wind. And then, ever so slowly, it crawled back into the dark seclusion of the woods. And then it was gone.

Paul stood frozen to the ground. Sam beside him. He wasn't sure how many minutes, or was it only seconds, had passed. But then he realized the woman was looking at him. Not at him. Through him. Not through him as though he wasn't there, but through him as though she could see all of his thoughts, his memories, his dreams, his prayers. It took a moment for him to realize that he could see through her too. He knew. He knew something... some question was answered there in the cool wind that had now become a slight breeze, some question he had yet to even ask. He couldn't quite grasp it, couldn't quite see it, but it was there. And seeing the woman and dog in front of him like that, so close they were a part of each other, brought a sense of peace to his heart, to his mind, and to his soul.

* * * * *

Suddenly there was a sharp twist to his left arm. Paul gave out a shout and abruptly sat up in bed. "What? A dream? No way! That wasn't just a dream. No way!"

He reached down and felt for Sam. Sam was right there on the floor beside the bed licking Paul's left hand.

"Did you wake me up, boy? You really gave me a start!" Paul ruffled the dog's thick coat, thinking nothing

Amy J. Cooper

of the leaves entangled in the fur as he gently pulled them free.

"But Faith like a jackal, feeds among the tombs, and even from these dead doubts she gathers her most vital hope."

*Herman Melville -
Moby Dick (1819-1891)*

Chapter 10

He was a big man. This could have been an attractive feature, but in his case it wasn't. It didn't make Larry appear masculine. It made him look like a weekend athlete "wannabe." Sure, he dieted. But then he would turn around and eat sweets all day and even sprinkle a packet or two of sugar in his water. This could add up fast since Larry bragged of the 8 glasses of water and more that he drank each day. He also bragged that he ran every day. Maybe he did. His body appeared otherwise, though.

Larry had a big face. It wasn't particularly attractive, although Larry thought it was. He had dark, curly hair that was always the subject of jokes.

"Hey, Larry, when did you get your hair permed?"

It was naturally curly. Or so Larry always grunted in answer.

It wasn't that Larry was the innocent victim in these ribbings. He wasn't. He was much, much worse. He was a born-again Christian. Granted, there are born-again Christians who really are good and behave as kind and loving children of God. But then there are those "born-agains" like Larry. Larry would use his "factual" knowledge of the Bible to harass his coworkers and neighbors. It was bad enough that he judged others, but what was worse was that he did it in the name of the Lord. Well, Larry said he did it in the Lord's name, but he knew that was far from the truth. The plastic crucifix that he hung from his rearview mirror in his old beat-up Chevrolet was hung upside down.

He had no excuses, which made him more evil. It wasn't like you could say he had been abused as a child and didn't know any better. Larry's mother was an angel. His father was just as pure in heart. Together they provided Larry with a beautiful, warm and loving childhood. His sister took after their parents. It would always make Larry want to puke when he thought about his sugar-coated family. And even though that was his reality, he wasn't going to have anything to do with that sweet stuff.

He got as far away from it as possible. And he didn't waste any time either. By the time Larry turned 13, he had discovered the other side was much more fun. It wasn't that he completely gave himself to Satan. He could only give in so much. You see, Larry liked to be the ruler. He wanted to be the king. So he gave what he could for the evil cause. And actually, as far as those who had felt the wrath of Larry were concerned, that was more than enough to get the message across. Once, when Larry was a young adult, his sister felt this wrath in a way that would affect her the rest of her life.

Early in life, Regina showed the rest of the world what true beauty was. From the time she was a young girl, she had already become the image of the long, slender beauty she would be as an adult. Her long

Wicked Dreams

black hair would glisten in the sun. Her pale skin would turn to a soft light brown after long summers playing under the warmth of that day star. But her physical beauty compared none to her soul. Regina was a soft, warm and loving spirit. She loved all creatures and anyone who was touched by her warm love would feel that touch for the rest of their lives. She gave freely of herself with only one selfish mar. Or at least to Regina it was a selfish mar.

You see, Regina was born with long, strong legs and elegant arms that failed to show the muscular strength they beheld. She was a born dancer. Her parents had recognized this when Regina first began to walk, and they enrolled her in dance classes as soon as she was ready. Not just any dance class would do either. They wrote their monthly checks payable to Madam Ruby McCallister. Sometimes when those monthly checks were difficult to write, Madam Ruby would insist that she needed Regina to help with the backstage design of a set or the ticket sales of an upcoming performance. For this, how could she take payment from Regina's parents? Why, she owed them! So Regina's lessons would not incur a charge that month. Truth be told, Madam Ruby adored this child and found her heart warmed when these arrangements allowed her to spend more time with the young ballerina.

As much as Regina loved ballet, she worried and worried that she was a selfish girl. She knew her parents sometimes found it difficult to pay for her lessons. She also knew Madam Ruby was making special arrangements to help her to continue her lessons. Regina knew all of this. It ate at her every day. Yet she couldn't bring herself to quit the classes.

Amy J. Cooper

Although Madam Ruby said Regina gave a special gift to others when they had the privilege of watching her dance, that didn't hold any meaning for Regina. You see, dance was the only thing that Regina did for herself. The thought that others experienced joy when they watched her dance never occurred to Regina. For the truth be told, even if no one would ever watch her dance again, she would dance and dance and dance. Oh, how her heart would soar as she would leap into the air! She was only dancing for her. This was her one selfish vice. A vice that to some would seem trivial, but to Larry it was everything. This would be how he would get her. This would be the door to her demise. All he had to do was turn the knob a little, give a slight push, and then step in. Oh, and would he ever step in. *Step? Hell no! It would be more of a charge. And little "sister tutu" would never know what hit her.*

"The devil is an angel too."

*- Miguel de Unamuno
(1864- 1936)*

Chapter 11

Larry labored long and hard to make his dream come true. First he had to get a job after school to save the money he would need. He couldn't believe how stupid his parents were because they really believed he was finally getting his act together and wanted to help the family out. They were relieved, actually, because Larry was 19 and about to graduate from high school. They had begun to think he would always be trouble.

"Well, they were right about that," Larry thought to himself as he walked home from the Quicky Burger where he had been working for the last year. "Oh, yeah, they were definitely right about that."

At first Larry thought he wouldn't be able to pull off his plan. It's pretty hard for a young kid in a small town to find out about the important stuff in life like how to hire a hit man. He had to be careful about how he went about his inquiries too, because he was always being watched.

Geezzus, ever since I killed old man Carver's dog the gawd damn sheriff has been after my butt. They never did prove nuttin though. They knew. Yeah, they knew. They just chose to not really believe it. Yeah, it was pretty gruesome. Almost more'n I could take. Man, the blood…..

Larry wouldn't admit it, but there was more to it than the fact that the sheriff was always watching him. Something had gone really haywire with the dogs in town. They all seemed to be watching him closely. *Man, I'm going crazy. There ain't no way those stupid dogs are watching me. Must be my guilty conscience.* And with that Larry let out a haunting laugh. For those who heard it, it didn't sound anything like a laugh. The birds in the nearby trees took flight, some screaming as they disappeared into the night air. A wild breeze came down through the path he was walking on, carrying some kind of foul smell that really didn't bother Larry at all. And the moon was covered by a cloud that suddenly appeared in what had been a cloudless sky. All of this happened as Larry walked and cackled to himself. All of this unnoticed by the young man who was slowly losing any hold of the small ounce of humanity that had managed to remain within his soul.

The activity that Larry's outburst had created escaped his attention except for one thing. He found himself startled by some movement in the trees. *Is there something in those trees?* It wasn't that Larry was scared per say, it was just that he was a bit anxious. And Larry wasn't used to being on this side of anxiety.

Suddenly something in the sky caught his attention. He looked up to see the full moon. He didn't remember that a cloud had just been over it, but somehow he had sensed that it wasn't glowing a moment ago. *Huh?* And then his eyes scanned the sky until they reached Orion. He lifted his right hand to the sky and pointed

Wicked Dreams

his index finger forming his hand into the shape of a gun. *Pow pow pow. Take that Orion. Regina loves ya' so you're dead. Bang! Bang!*

Thinking of Regina made Larry smile. He didn't really have a nice smile either. When he smiled, his brown teeth showed and his eyes took on a crazy look. He somewhat resembled one of those scary rubber masks that kids wore on Halloween when they went trick-or-treating. He knew this. And he was so twisted in his vanity that he thought he had a *darn nice smile*. He was "smiling" now because he was thinking about Regina and what would be happening to her soon, very soon. He just needed to save up for a couple more months and then he could buy *her little present*. He had already met the man who would do it.

Larry kind of liked Spike. He was way cool with his pierced nose, ear, eyebrow, tongue and who knew what else. That would be cool to Larry only because he knew how many infections Spike had to deal with to maintain his cool look. Still, there was the hair that was his namesake. Yep, it was molded into three spikes on the top of his head with gawd-only-knew how many gallons of hair gel and spray. Most people would look at Spike and try to tell him that his hair wasn't cool anymore, but not Larry. Larry was one of the few people who knew the truth about Spike's hair. It wasn't for looks, man. It was for keeps. *Killing for keeps. Arrr Arr Arrr. Way funny, man.* Spike actually had slender, sharp metal rods in those spikes. Yes, few people other than Larry knew the truth about Spike's hair, but they would never say anything. *Dead men don't talk, man. Arrr Arrr Arr.*

Amy J. Cooper

Larry was still "laughing" to himself when he reached home. He ran up the front porch steps and through the front door. He walked through the living room where his family had gathered eating popcorn and watching some stupid movie. He gladly ignored them as they greeted him and asked him to join them. Up the stairs he trotted and into his room, slamming the door behind him.

*"Our interest's on the dangerous edge of things,
The honest thief, the tender murderer..."*

-Robert Browning (1812-1889)

Chapter 12

Well, he had the money. Well, not really. *Not anymore*, Larry grinned to himself. Spike had the money. Good old Spike. Spike thought of everything. Why wouldn't he? After all, he was a professional. He'd been in prison before and everything. Now he was living in a quiet little ghost town just about 30 miles south called Ravenwood. Spike was pretty radical for that little town, but still, living with his mother kept his parole officer off his back. What trouble could he get into in a little sleepy town? *Plenty.*

Larry had been meeting Spike on and off for the last several months, but last night was special because he paid his whole debt in advance. He had brought a Picture of Regina's friend, Betsy, with him. He gave Spike all of the details about where Regina practiced her stupid ballet and what nights of the week she could be found there. She was there on Saturdays too, but Spike didn't care about that. It had to be night, when it was dark. He didn't want the light of day to mess up his job. All the details set, Larry had one last question for Spike.

"When 'ya gonna do it, man?"
"Ain't telling 'ya!"

"Geezus, man! I paid good money!"

"It's for your own protection, man!"

"What in the hell are you talking about?"

"Man, if I tell you when I'm gonna do it, you'll be all weird act'n that day and then people will think you did it no matter how good an alibi you got."

"Man, Spike, I'm sorry! You're right! You're the man! You're the man!"

"Yeah, that's right, kid. Stick with me I'll teach 'ya things. But you gotta wait. I can't be seen with 'ya until way after the deed is done. Cool?"

"Yeah, that's cool. How will I know when I can see you again, man?"

"You'll know when you see me, man. I'll find you when it's cool."

And with that the two parted ways, Larry grinning as he walked to his car. Spike, walking with a slight limp, headed in the other direction, Regina's picture clutched in his hand.

Larry kept up his daily routine for the next several weeks and slowly became less anxious. Actually, he was kind of relieved because all of his work was done. Waiting turned out to be much easier than he thought it was going to be.

And then one night it happened. Larry knew it was happening because it was 8:30 at night and little *sister tutu* wasn't home yet. He wished he could drive down there and see for himself, but Spike had warned him back in the beginning that would be stupid. So he waited. He waited and waited.

Someone else was waiting across town. It was little Betsy. She had borrowed her mother's car to take her and her best friend Regina to ballet class that night.

Wicked Dreams

Afterward, they were going to go out for pizza. It was fun being a ballerina at this age because they were growing and they were dancing so hard every day that they got to eat everything they wanted. They had both been warned that it wouldn't always be this way. One day, they would have to struggle to keep those fat grams from adding up. But for now, their growing bodies were eating up the pizza just as fast as the girls could gobble it down.

Finally, Betsy got out of the car and ran back into the old brick building and up the steps. She found Regina in the upstairs hallway talking to some stranger. He was kind of cute. He was a lot older than them and in a suit like what Betsy had seen in the window of Larramy's, that expensive men's clothing store. Regina and the strange man were deep in conversation when Betsy approached them.

She startled them when she spoke, "Are you coming, Regina?"

"I'm sorry, Betsy! Yeah! I'll be right there. This is Mr. Anderson . He's come all the way from New York City because he heard about me! Can you believe it! He's offering me a scholarship! Regina was out of breath as she tried to explain her delay to her friend.

"Excuse me," the handsome man in the grey suit spoke. "Would you mind, please, waiting for us downstairs? I promise I will only keep your friend a moment more."

Betsy was excited for her friend, but a little put off by the way the man had disregarded her. "Yeah, I'll go wait in the car." She was pouting a little as she went down the stairs and out to her mother's car. But once she sat inside, started the engine and tuned in the radio, she started feeling good again. She was a good friend to Regina, the kind of friend who wouldn't be jealous over something like this. In fact, she was actually getting pretty excited. Regina really deserved going to New York. She was definitely the best ballerina Madam Ruby had ever had in class. The best this side of the Mississippi, Madam Ruby always said.

Betsy was so caught up in her excited thoughts about her friend's good fortune that she hadn't noticed the shadow that had suddenly emerged from her back seat. She didn't even hear a sound as the gloved hands came over the front seat and wrapped a rope around her slender throat. No time to scream, no moment to panic; for as wicked as Spike was, he felt some tenderness towards young girls. Yes, he would do the job and earn his money. After all, he was a man who kept his word and earned his keep. But he also felt some link to young girls. Maybe it was because of his little sister who had died of leukemia when she was only 15. For whatever reason, he showed mercy to Betsy, killing her so cleanly and quickly that she didn't have time to be scared or feel pain.

Sleep little darlin'. Sleep my little angel. Spike quickly slid from the back seat, out the door, away from the car, and ever so silently ran down the back alleyway.

Mr. Anderson looked at his watch and suddenly grew impatient with Regina. He didn't seem to care anymore about the answers she gave to his multitude of questions. He didn't even want to stick around for her to give him an audition. He pretty much blew her off and said he would call her as he ran down the stairs and out the door.

Regina's feelings were hurt, but she convinced herself that it was only because Mr. Anderson was a busy man. Soon the excitement filled her heart again. She grabbed her duffel bag and ran down the stairs to meet her waiting friend. She couldn't wait to talk to Betsy. Betsy was such a great friend. She would truly be happy for Regina and not jealous like some of the other girls in her class would be.

But when Regina reached the bottom of the stairs and pushed open the glass door, she saw something that confused her. *Why was the back door of Betsy's mother's car standing open? Why was Betsy taking a nap with her head resting on the steering wheel?* These questions were running over and over again through Regina's mind as she approached the car. She was already trembling when she pulled on the door handle. Slowly she opened the car door. Everything was moving in slow motion just like it does in bad dreams. *This is a bad dream. This is really just bad dream. It's a dream..... it's a ...* and then she fainted, hitting her head on the door frame as her body slumped over into a heap on the pavement.

*"Care-charmer Sleep, son of the sable Night,
Brother to Death, in silent darkness born."*

-*Samuel Daniel (1562-1619)*

Chapter 13

She heard sounds. Some of them were familiar to her, some were not. But all of them confused her. She felt someone holding her hand, but she couldn't open her eyes to see who it was. She really wanted to, though, because the touching of her hand gave her such great comfort that she really wanted to thank whoever it was. But before she could focus any more attention on the stranger who held her hand, she would drift off again, lost in her dreams.

The dreams would always start out the same. She would walk down the stairs of the ballet school. Then she would open the door, step out onto the sidewalk and see the car that belonged to the mother of her best friend. She would walk slowly toward the car, anxious to talk to Betsy. She would open the door, but Betsy wouldn't be there. Sometimes no one would be there at all. But the worst dreams were when something was there, something so horrid that Regina would open her mouth to scream, but was so terrified she couldn't even let out a squeak. It was something so awful, so frightening, that when Regina turned to run, her legs moved in slow motion, moving slower and slower until

Wicked Dreams

her feet seemed to melt into the concrete sidewalk and she couldn't even move at all. There were good dreams too. The dreams that made Regina feel the best were the ones when Betsy was there. She was glowing, surrounded by a pool of light, and smiling sweetly at Regina as she floated up through the car roof and into the night air.

"I will always be watching you, Regina. Don't be sad. I am so very happy. Don't be sad."

One time when Regina had a dream like this she woke to find herself crying and was frightened to discover someone else in the room with her. She was even more scared when she realized who it was.

"Larry, what are you doing in here?"

"Hey, baby sister," Larry whispered as he wiped the tears from Regina's eyes.

"What are you doing? Why are you here?" Although Regina loved her brother, she was very afraid of him and tried to never be alone with him. There was something about him that was evil, something she wanted no part of.

"Oh, baby sister; I just came to see you. We're alike now, you know, you and me are alike."

"How can you say that? We've never been anything alike," Regina answered, her throat scratchy from days of not speaking.

"Oh, yes we are, little Sister Tutu. Oh, yes we are."

"Don't call me that! We are not alike!" Regina screamed, although it sounded more like a whimper.

"Well, little Sister Tutu, we are. You see, we both look out for number one. And that is the only way to be. Yep, that's the way smart people do it."

Amy J. Cooper

"I'm not like that!"

"Well, then, why weren't you there to protect your little friend, Betsy? Huh? What kept you from being there with her so she didn't have to die? Were 'ya helping some poor old person with their groceries?"

"No."

"Were you helping Grandma Wilkins to cross the street?"

"No! I wasn't. Shut up!"

"Well, then just what was keeping you from your dear sweet, and definitely dead, friend, my dear?"

"Oh, my gawd! It was that man! It was Mr. Anderson!" Regina gasped.

"And just what about him, sister dear?"

"I was talking to him and Betsy was waiting outside for me."

"Were you talking about helping Betsy go to that stupid school she's always jabbering about in New York?"

"No! It was about me! He wanted to talk to me! Oh, my gawd!"

"Yep! There you have it little sister! You were looking out for numero uno while little friend Betsy was out breathing her last breath. Yep! We are just alike. I would have said screw her too, if she would have been standing in the way of me getting my dream. Yep. We are just alike."

"No we're not! No, we're not! No, we're not! Regina screamed as everything faded to black and she slid back into a deep sleep that would envelope her for three more days.

"Nothing in the world is single,
All things by a law divine,
In one spirit meet and mingle"

- Percy Bysshe Shelley (1792-1822)

Chapter 14

She missed Emily. Emily was the only person she enjoyed running with. *Uh, Dianna, Emily's a dog!* Well, at any rate, there weren't many "others" that Dianna would share her running with. True, she didn't like the distraction when she was concentrating on her breathing. Asthmatics were picky about things like that. But it was more than that. Running was something that stirred Dianna's soul.

The road was a soft asphalt that absorbed some of the shock to Dianna's legs. She liked that, but she would trade it with hard cement tomorrow. She learned early in her running days that you need to combine as many different surfaces in your training as possible. Not only did it help to relieve some of the stress that one-surface running could put on the legs, but it also prepared you for whatever changes in surface you may encounter on race day.

It was early in the morning. She was breathing clearly, and she didn't feel like she was fighting a migraine. Those were her only two enemies, both painful, but only one deadly. And both were in hiding on this fine summer morning. The air was damp and warm and the road was still a little wet from the early morning rain. This was Dianna's favorite time to run, right after a rain. She lifted her head into the wind and caught the fragrance of the soil. She was aware of the sounds of the birds in the nearby trees as they chatted and flew about. She could smell the warmth of the sun as it dried the grass in the meadows nearby. This morning world was hers alone. She knew that Emily would have loved this run. But since this was a long one, 18 miles, she didn't bring her along. She didn't want to subject Emily to what torture a run like that could bring. Plus, she didn't want to carry two water bottles on her hip holster when she was running that far. She learned that early on too. Whatever felt the least bit uncomfortable in the beginning of a run would feel 100 times worse when you were covering that kind of mileage.

When Dianna would get back to the cabin, she would take Emily for a nice long walk. It would be good for both of them. Dianna liked to stretch her legs out that way following a run like this one, and she knew Emily would enjoy the adventure. Ever since they had come out here to The Meadows, a place she had heard about from a fellow writer, Dianna with Emily had enjoyed many an interesting adventure.

Dianna had gone freelance just a few short months ago and was really enjoying the freedom it gave her. She could write until all hours of the night draped in her warm, cozy, red flannel robe and fuzzy slippers, and then she could have her days free, or vice versa, depending on which direction her writing mania took that day. Emily noticed the difference in her master and was enjoying it too.

Wicked Dreams

As these thoughts were going through Dianna's head and she began her last mile, headed home, Emily was watching. True, Emily was back at the cabin lying on the thick rug in the center of the living room, but she was also with Dianna. This wasn't the first time that Emily had traveled in her dreams to be with her master. In fact, sometimes she traveled with that man, the man that made her master smile. She still had a clear memory of his scent even though much time had passed since she had been near him in the real world. And the scent was slowly getting stronger. Emily was smiling in her sleep and her tail began to wag as the scent of the good man grew even stronger.

Dianna was pumping her arms higher and harder as she neared the end of her run. This was a trick she had learned from her beloved high school track coach. The harder and higher you pump your arms, the harder your legs will follow. She was running hard and fast and she loved this part best of all. It was as close as she could come to flying. This was just like how it was in her running dreams. She was always surprised by the strength she felt when she ran, especially when she kicked like this after such a long run. Just as she reached her 18 mile goal and slowed down her stride, gently easing down to a walk, a motorcycle sped past her. Unaccustomed to sharing this country back road with traffic, she looked up in time to see the brake lights of the bike flash. She thought the man on the bike was looking at her through the side mirror, but she couldn't be certain.

Might be some jerk, Dianna. Better get on back to the cabin.

As Dianna headed off the road to take a hidden path to the cabin she had discovered days earlier, the bike slowed to a stop and began to turn around. Dianna had no idea the bike was slowly creeping back in her direction as she disappeared into the trees. When she reached the cabin, she stepped in and found Emily stretched out on the rug, wagging her tail and wearing a smile. *Wonder if she's dreaming about her knight in shining armor?*

The scent of the man was at its strongest now and Emily could see him clearly. He was on one of those two-wheeled machines that made a lot of noise and moved fast. But he wasn't moving fast now. He was sitting in the middle of the road looking into the woods. Emily knew that place where he was. She knew where he was looking. She knew it was the path that she and her master had discovered between the cabin and the road. She could tell the man was confused, that he didn't see the path. That didn't worry Emily though. He was near. That was enough for now.

Emily stopped wagging her tail as she picked up another scent. She couldn't comprehend what that smell was. It was oddly familiar, but yet it was still strange. In her dream, she seemed to fly over the bike. As she hovered over top of it, she noticed something moving in the little compartment that was connected to the bike. She didn't know that humans called that thing a sidecar, but she did know there was something inside it, something living. Suddenly a head popped up, and to Emily's amazement and delight she was looking down at the most beautiful long yellow mane she had ever seen. Her tail began to thump loudly on the rug as she looked down at the most beautiful male she had ever seen. He looked up at her as though he could see her. His tail began to wag.

"What's up, girl? Are you having a good dream this time?" Dianna softly spoke as she rubbed Emily's pink belly.

"What's up, Sam? Do you like it here? Wanna' stay?"

Sam wagged his tail in response and Paul turned the bike around to follow the signs that promised The Meadows cabins were very near.

*"When the footpads quail at the night-bird's wail,
and black dog's bay at the moon,
Then is the specters' holiday – then is the ghosts' high noon!"*

- Sir William Schwenck Gilbert (1836-1911)

Chapter 15

It was late at night. The woods were only lit by the grace of the full moon. Dianna was running and she could feel Emily running along beside her, but she could only catch glimpses of her when there was a clearing in the trees that allowed the moonlight to push back the shadows. She was fighting panic and could feel impending defeat as her lungs grew heavier and heavier. *Not now! Gawd not now!*

Emily knew the fear her master felt. But she had known this fear before. It was important to somehow let her master know that she was not alone. That would give her courage and would keep her from making those strange wheezing sounds. She could sense when those sounds were near, and she was picking up on them now.

Just as Emily was wondering how to get through to her master, they reached another clearing in the trees. Dianna suddenly stopped running and clutched her chest. Her lungs were filled with phlegm and were so tight that only a minimum amount of air was getting through. She shook her inhaler, poised to use it, but waited. What good was it to waste a shot of medicine when her lungs would not accept it? *If I can just stop panicking, I can get a shot in and I'll be okay.*

She looked down into Emily's face and was confused by the expression she saw as the night shadows danced about Emily's muzzle. Emily lifted her head into the night air, staring up at the full moon. She began to sing a long, haunting howl that would have sent chills up Dianna's spine any other time. But for some strange reason, this lowly howl brought comfort to Dianna. She felt the tension leaving her body. The panic was leaving too and her lungs began to open up, ever so slightly. It was enough for her to shoot in a dose from her inhaler and her lungs were instantly gratified. She coughed and spit out some of the phlegm that was drowning her lungs. Even though she was feeling a little better, she knew things were still not right. She felt stronger, but still had the sense that whatever they were running away from was still chasing them.

Emily saw that her master was getting stronger. She could sense the wheezing leaving her master's chest. And she was thankful that the Huntress of the Moon had not let her down. She glanced up into the sky to offer a prayer of thanks, when she was suddenly granted one more favor. The moon was suddenly clouded over and Emily and Dianna were standing in pitch-black darkness in the deep of the woods. Although it may not seem like a favor to any outsider, this darkness was indeed a blessing, for the evil thing was just a few yards away. It had been chasing the two females for about a mile without any problem. The night moon was full and lit the way. It was confused that the moon was gone now. And it wasn't sure where the two were anymore.

As the evil predator stopped to try to understand what was happening, Emily and Dianna were having another encounter. They had picked up on the fowl smell that was wafting towards them, and Dianna was fighting the compulsion to vomit, coughing up more and more phlegm. And then, something else was there with them. Dianna slowly stood up just as she felt something brush past her face. There it was again, and again. Even though the darkness hid everything from her vision, somehow Dianna knew that the soft-lit things she felt were butterfly wings. And somehow, just knowing that, she felt stronger and ready for whatever was about to come. She could feel Emily beside her, and that gave her great comfort too.

But there was someone else in the woods. Dianna wasn't sure how she knew that, but she did. She thought she could feel Emily wagging her tail. *You feel it too, don't you, honey?* Dianna thought, too afraid to speak out loud.

And then a whisper came to her in the darkness, "It's all right. Sam and I are here too. Together we can do this. And Sam says there are more. And then, there are the butterflies. Yes, the butterflies."

Just as Dianna was trying to remember where she had heard that voice before, she realized that the fluttering wings were no longer brushing her cheeks. *Where did they go?*

The answer Dianna was looking for was only a few yards away. In the darkness, the butterflies had flown over to where the beast had been waiting for

Wicked Dreams

the moonlight to return. They fluttered about his head, but they did not offer him strength. They offered him fear. Fear was not something he often felt. He didn't know what the fluttering was that he felt about his face and neck, but it was making him lose focus on the hunt. The flutterings were making him want to turn the other way. The feeling wasn't so strong that he would actually leave, but it was confusing him enough that he stood still not sure what to do.

In the silence of the darkness, Dianna heard a sound. It was another dog offering a lonely howl to the night sky. She turned to Emily and was surprised to find that Emily was lying in the bed beside her.

"There is no way that was a dream!"

The steady rhythm of a wagging tail was the only answer Dianna received.

And just about a half a mile away, there on the porch of another cabin, sat Sam. He lifted his head up toward the moon and let out another howl. The sound woke Paul who had fallen exhausted on an old wooden rocker on the porch. He was confused when he realized where he was. He was surprised because he was so very sure he had just been in the woods with that woman and her dog.

Sam meandered over to his master and licked his hand as if to say he understood.

"Thanks, boy. That helps. Let's go inside and get a bite to eat."

Sam answered by thumping his tail against Paul's leg and then galloping through the open door and into the warm, softly lit cabin.

That night, as Sam and Paul dozed in their cabin and Dianna and Emily slept in theirs, there was much activity in the woods and nearby meadows. Had there been any taxonomists in the woods that night, and had the moon allowed them to see, they would have been astounded by the display of butterflies that fluttered about. The colorful wings beautifully danced about each other as if in celebration of something that was yet to come.

And in the nearby meadows there were other creatures stirring. These came on all fours. Some came alone, some came in pairs, but somehow they all found each other and in a place in the meadow as close as you could get to the woods without going in them, these beautiful dogs cuddled up against one another and began to wearily drift off to sleep. Unlike the butterflies, the dogs had an air of apprehension about them. One or two of them offered a song to the moon as the rest settled down to their dreams.

*Speak to Him thou for He hears, and
Spirit with Spirit can meet-
Closer is He than breathing, and nearer
than hands and feet.*

*-Alfred, Lord Tennyson
(1809-1892)*

Chapter 16

Dianna was in that place between the real world and the dream world. She was aware that her arms were around Emily and her face was buried in her warm soft fur. *How odd that Emily's fur feels so incredibly snugly soft and yet if I get just one of those hairs in my foot, it's like a splinter.* Dianna's thoughts drifted back to just a few days ago when she had felt a sharp pain in her foot and had to stop and drop right down on the side of the road. She couldn't get her running shoe and sweaty sock off fast enough. And there to her surprise she saw a single white hair stuck straight into the ball of her foot. *What the hell?* She had to work the hair out like you would a small sliver of wood. And the relief was instantaneous.

Dianna remembered that morning vividly. And the thought of how wonderful yesterday's run had been, (*after that great big deadly hair was pulled from her foot*). What was it about that motorcycle that haunted her? She couldn't think of anybody she knew who rode... not since she was a kid. And then she drifted off to sleep again thinking about the stepbrother she hadn't seen for over 20 years. His name was Greg and he rode a 1968 BSA. Even though Dianna was still a young girl then, she was old enough to appreciate the beauty of the bike. She was also old enough to appreciate the way her stepbrother treated her. She had really seen him only one other time before that morning...that morning...ahhh, that morning. He had ridden up the street and into her driveway. He had a friend on the back, some other guy who was pretty cute for an older guy. Dianna thought Greg was pretty cute too, for a stepbrother, but more than that, she thought he was awfully nice. She knew that a sophisticated, older teenager who rode a motorcycle of his own, for gawd's sake, wouldn't normally have time for some lanky pre-teenage stepsister who'd never even seen a motorcycle before. But Greg was different. He saw something in Dianna's face and knew that she had that fire in her. That fire that would grow into a burning love for the ride of two wheels and the wind. He popped a helmet on her head and off they went. It may have only been around the block, but that ride has lasted Dianna a lifetime. It was the thrill of the ride and it was the kindness of a stepbrother she would never see again.

Why didn't I ever learn to ride? Dianna was wondering to herself as she slowly returned to the real world. But she didn't want to return to the real world. Something was pulling her in. *Something or someone?* Dianna wasn't sure; she only knew that she felt this sense of urgency to not go wherever it was she was headed.

Ever so slowly, Dianna opened her eyes. At first she felt relieved, and truthfully, a bit silly, because she was right there in her cabin and the soft morning sunlight was just beginning to drift through the window. *Hold on, Dianna... something's just not quite right here...*

Dianna's eyes moved cautiously around the walls of the room until they suddenly stopped at the corner near the window. Her eyes grew large as the hair on her arms began to stand up. *There is something in the shadows there. There is someone in here with me! Oh, my gawd!* After staring for a moment, Dianna realized that she was looking at the figure of a man. It didn't seem quite real, partly because he was so very, very ugly, but also because, although he was enough of a presence to scare the hell out of her, Dianna had the feeling that he wasn't truly there. He had dark curly hair and a big face and eyes that looked like they had seen hell, had visited there awhile, and had liked it. And there was the smell. *What was that foul smell?*

As quickly as the image had materialized before her, it was gone. A cool breeze gently tossed her bedroom curtain about. There were a few butterflies hanging around just outside the window. Although Dianna was still a little upset about what she had just seen in her room, she found comfort in the brilliant purplish blue colored wings in flight. *What kind of butterfly is that?*

Dianna heard a moan next to her and turned to look at Emily who was also staring out the window. Her brow was furrowed as though she was in deep thought. And she was. She had awoken to discover that a presence had been made and that she had not been forewarned. It worried her that she had not seen it first. *Why did her master see it first?* She was apprehensive that she would not be the right guard for her master. And as she watched the dancing purple wings, she felt comfort. *There was a reason for that. I don't need to know what that one looks like yet. It was for her, for her master that the presence needed to be made. This is how it should be.*

"Hey, girl! Today's a short one! Wanna' do a few miles with me?"

Emily responded with a hearty wag of her tail and a great big lick on Dianna's face.

"Ooooh, Honey! Brush your teeth before you do that! Okay?"

Then the two joined in a wrestling match that ended with them both on the floor, Dianna laughing hysterically and Emily with a big grin and tail wagging strong.

They had a light breakfast and headed out for a run. Up the hidden path and through the woods toward the road they went. The air was fresh and clear with just a hint of dewy dampness. *Perfect.* Dianna was already feeling the spiritual cleansing that a good run always gave her. *Not bad for only ¼ a mile!* Emily was running happily along next to her. They were both free from any scary thoughts of things that go bump in the night. This was a new day. And boy did it feel good.

Dianna could see the clearing up ahead where they would cut through the meadow and then on to the road. She loved that road, but she also loved the way her feet felt running on this path. Even through her orthotics and the thick layer of rubbery cushion on the bottom of her shoes she was still very aware of the soft earth that her feet were padding along. In the few short days that she had been running that path, she felt she had come to memorize it. There was the part where it dipped down a little. Up here was where there was a slight decline to the left. These were things that

Wicked Dreams

you wouldn't notice if you were just walking on the path or if you were just looking at it. These were things you would only know if you had been running on it and really feeling it with your feet, really experiencing it. Emily must have been thinking the same thing as they both ran toward the left side of the path so that when they rounded that sharp curve ahead, they wouldn't trip on the old rotten tree branch that lay there. *Oh, Emily we are such a good team!*

Out of the woods and through the meadow they ran. Two companions who couldn't be more happy to spend time together. Free spirits running for the sake of running. They reached the road and started heading toward the town. Sometimes, on these short runs they would go into Rose's Diner and have a snack. The folks in town and Rose had already become accustomed to the pair and weren't offended by the sweaty runners coming in for a break. In fact, the town folk often encouraged the two, cheering them on. Someone would always go back into Rose's kitchen and fetch a big bowl of water for Emily while Rose would make up some frozen fruit concoction for Dianna.

Up the road they ran, side by side. Just a mile ahead they could see the outskirts of town. *Well, the whole town is outskirts if you think about it. Don't blink...* Dianna giggled to herself. She thought it was funny, but truth be told, this little town tugged at her heartstrings and she was thrilled to be a part of it.

"There they are baby! They must have figured out our training schedule!"

There in front of the diner were a few of Dianna and Emily's fans. She could make out the red flannel shirt that had to belong to old man Fred. And there was that blue baseball cap. That has to be Dan. And that smaller one must be Patty.

"Come on Emily! Let's give them something to cheer about!" With that the two broke their pace and kicked like the wind, dust flying behind them. Dianna, pumping her arms, was strong and swift, but no competition for the sleek skill of Emily. The dog reached the diner, and with tail still moving a mile a minute was bathing in the petting from her fans. Just a few seconds later, Dianna reached the small crowd.

"Yahoo, Little Lady! You'll win that race for sure!" Fred shouted, forgetting that he was the only of them who was hard of hearing.

"Fred, I keep telling you, I win just by finishing. It's not that kind of race for me. I just want to do my 26¼ miles and go out to dinner when I'm done."

"That dinner better be here or I'll be sorely disappointed."

Dianna looked up into Rose's smiling face. The two had become buddies from the moment they met. Rose was just a little bit older and wiser than Dianna, but Dianna had her share of city stories that helped her to keep up. Rose wiped her hands on her apron and reached up to tie her black wavy hair into a ponytail.

"Get on in here! I've got one of those fruit smoothies with your name on it."

When Dianna and Emily stepped inside the diner, they were so preoccupied with their friends that they didn't notice the man who sat back in the corner booth. But he noticed them. His jaw dropped and his eyes opened wide in surprise. *Oh my gawd! It's her! It's Dianna! She's here! How can that be?*

His eyes dropped to the floor where Emily was snuggling up on the rug that had been laid just for her. *Must be one special dog if they let her in here, in a restaurant.*

Rose came over to Paul as though she could read his thoughts.

"Hope the dog doesn't bother you. We do things a little different here. We treat dogs like people. Although that may be a little condescending to them, they don't seem to be bothered by it much."

"No, I don't mind. I should have brought Sam."

"Well, bring this Sam fellow with you tomorrow and we'll show him how a dog's breakfast should be made."

"Thanks! I will. Hey, that lady there, is her name Dianna?"

"Why, yes, it is! Do you know her from the city?"

"Well, it's been quite a while. We dated a few times and then... well, I guess I don't know what happened, but I haven't seen her for..."

"Well, we can fix that! You can see her just fine now! Get off your butt and I'll serve your pancakes over there at her table."

Paul looked up into Rose's kind face. She could see the panic in his eyes.

"Oh, for gawd's sake! She won't bite 'ya!"

Before Paul was even aware that he had stood up and walked over to Dianna's table, he found himself standing in front of her and looking down into her beautiful sweaty face.

"Oh, my gawd! Paul! Is it really you? What are you doing here?"

"I was about to ask you the same thing!"

And then the two were lost in conversation. They talked through big, sloppy bites of blueberry pancakes unaware that there had gathered a small crowd at Rose's, a small crowd of gentle smiling faces.

"Ain't love grand?" Patty whispered. She was answered by a few "Um-hums" and a couple slurping sounds as Fred downed his third cup of coffee.

"And I to my motorcycle
Parked like the soul of the junkyard
Restored, a bicycle fleshed
With power, and tore off
Up Highway 106, continually
Drunk on the wind in my mouth,
Wringing the handlebar for speed,
Wild to be wreckage forever."

- James Dickey (1923-1997)

Chapter 17

She was trembling uncontrollably. *I have no business being out here! What the hell am I doing?* She was unbearably hot even though the morning air was cool enough she could see her breath.

"Okay! This is it! Now, let's try to get into second gear this time. You can do it!"

"I think I can! I think I can! I think I can!" Dianna yelled out trying to masque her fear.

Very slowly, she eased out on the clutch and gave a slight nudge to the throttle. Eyes straight ahead, feet still on the ground, the bike began to inch forward. Slowly she gave the throttle more of a twist, let the clutch out a little more, and then she began to pick up speed. Dianna could hear Paul's voice in her head as she went through each step. They had started to talk about it last night and then this morning they had the real class work. He described everything to her as they sat next to the bike sipping coffee and munching on blueberry muffins from Rose's Diner. She had imagined herself really riding as they talked about it, but didn't believe it would actually ever happen. Now, here she was, just a few short hours later, feeling the slight wind toss her ponytail about. Even though the helmet was a little big, it still felt somewhat stifling. Still, as she pulled in the clutch and shifted into second gear with her left foot, she had the sensation she was flying. It was almost better than running because she didn't have to struggle to breathe. Almost better. *This is the next best thing to running!* She didn't think anything could come close to running, but here it was.

Okay, let's show Teacher I can do third too! She gained speed and just as Paul said would happen, she could actually feel the bike asking her to shift to third. *Oh, yeah! This is like when my body says kick it in, Dianna! Kick that last ¼ mile in!* So she pulled in the clutch with her left hand again and shifted into third gear with her left foot. *Smooth.*

And to Paul, she really did look smooth. *Ahhh, a natural!* They had talked about her taking the motorcycle enrichment class and that this was just practice before that, yet she seemed to already have a feel for balancing the bike and knowing when to shift. *Yeah, she looks smooth. Uh, well...* "What in the heck is she doing?"

At first Paul thought she was downshifting, slowing down to turn around and come back to him. But then she looked all wrong. She did a sort of slow weave and before his horrified eyes she went down.

"Dianna!" He screamed as he ran down the road toward her.

Wicked Dreams

Emily and Sam had been frolicking in the meadow and they both suddenly stopped and spun around to watch Paul running down the road. They had heard the way he had yelled out and understood the urgency of the call. They began running side by side down the road following Sam's master. Dianna was sitting on the road next to the bike, her head bent down and her shoulders shuddering.

When the threesome reached Dianna, Paul was beside himself with fear that she had been hurt. "Oh, Dianna! Oh, Baby! I'll get you to the hospital! Emily! Emily! Get away from her! What are you doing?"

Emily was licking Dianna's face with tail in full wag. Paul bent down closer to Dianna and suddenly realized why Emily was behaving the way she was. Dianna wasn't crying. She was laughing.

"You're okay?"

"Yeah, just a little bruised."

"What is so funny?"

"Well, I guess it wouldn't be to you, but the whole time I was falling, it went in slow motion and I could hear you in my head."

"What was I saying?' Paul asked as he dropped down to sit on the road next to her, feeling a bit more relieved than he did a moment ago.

"Well, you were saying, 'Don't look to the ground! Don't look to the ground! Remember you always go where your head is pointed."

"What is so funny about that?"

"You were right!"

"Huh?"

"Look where I landed! You were right!" Dianna burst out laughing again. Sam and Emily danced to the sound of Dianna's laughter and after a moment, Paul couldn't help but to join them. They would have looked odd to a stranger; a couple dogs and a couple humans laughing in the middle of the road next to a bike that was parked a bit oddly.

Yes, they would have looked odd to a stranger. That is to most any stranger. But they didn't look odd at all to Maggie. They didn't look odd because Maggie knew what was happening. She knew exactly what was happening. They were here for a reason. And they were becoming as one. This is what it looks like when two become joined in spirit and mind. Maggie knew that.

She gathered up her long, dirty skirt and turned to walk back through the field. Behind her walked a small train of dogs. Some looked pure breed, some a mysterious blend, some limping, some looking strong and young. They quietly followed her to the far end of the meadow, that place just at the edge of the woods. One or two of them glanced back at the foursome on the road and would wag their tail once or twice as if to say "so-long for now dear friend." And they slowly all gathered to eat the food Maggie had brought them and drink the cool water. After feeding them, petting them, and inspecting them for ticks, she turned back toward the road and slowly began to walk to her old beat-up Ford pickup truck that was parked so far down on the side of the road it was almost hidden amongst the weeds and bushes. The dogs watched her go and settled down in the field's tall weeds for a restful morning nap.

All of this happened without Paul or Dianna noticing any movement. They were engrossed in looking over the bike. Paul was more worried about Dianna than the bike, something he thought he'd never do. Dianna was more worried about the bike than her own slightly bruised body, something she thought she'd never do. And Sam and Emily were sitting side by side, tails slightly wagging, looking across the field, knowing that their new friends were getting nearer and nearer. Slowly, they each tilted their head a bit as if to listen to the wind. Slowly, they lifted their snouts to the air as if smelling a message in the breeze. And slowly their tails stopped wagging as they realized that the other one was drawing nearer too.

"The belief in a supernatural source of evil is not necessary; men alone are quite capable of every wickedness."

- *Joseph Conrad (1857-1924)*

Chapter 18

She could remember it so clearly, as though it happened only yesterday. She had been in the hospital for a few weeks before they let her come home. Regina slowly recovered, as much as one can, from the death of her best friend, but it was a difficult journey. That was the main reason she had been in the hospital for so long. She had been so distraught that she wouldn't eat and only wanted to sleep. Sometimes she didn't even want to sleep. Sometimes the dreams would be so horrifying that she was afraid to go back to sleep once she had been awoken by her own screams.

But slowly she came out of it. She was grateful to the psychiatrist and the nurses who had helped her get better. She realized now that a part of her would never completely recover from seeing her friend dead in the car that night. And she knew she would never be able to forgive herself. It was her fault Besty had died. If she hadn't been so selfish about talking to that man about a dancing scholarship, Betsy wouldn't have been waiting all alone outside.

No, she would never forgive herself. For punishment, she gave up her life's dream. When she stopped dancing, a part of her went numb. She grew

Wicked Dreams

withdrawn and painfully thin. She hid away in her parents' house until she finally went away to college. But not even college life could break her out of her shell. She studied hard, thankful for the distraction of her difficult classes. She never went out with friends. She slowly withdrew from the human race.

Today she was taking her lunch break outside in the park. It was a beautiful warm summer day and she enjoyed the smell of the grass and the song the leaves sang as they danced in the light summer breeze. She sat down on a bench in the shade and peeled open her brown bag lunch. Egg salad sandwich, apple and a thermos of ice-tea. Same meal she had every day. Methodically, she chewed a bite of sandwich and stared blankly into the flowerbed in front of her. Gradually, she realized that she was witnessing a sort of dance before her eyes. Two butterflies with the most amazing purple wings were fluttering about in the flowers just in front of Regina's bench. They were so close she almost felt she could touch them. She reached out her hand and one of the flying beauties landed in her palm and stayed there with wings gently moving back and forth.

As soon as the heavenly creature had landed in her palm, Regina's memory tossed her back to when she had been out of the hospital only about a week or so. She had gone for a walk in this same park. *Yes, and I was just over there when…*

"Hey, little sister! Whatcha' doin'?"

Frightened by the sudden appearance of her brother, Regina was not able to respond.

"Walk'n it off, heh? Are you walk'n it off? It must be hell trying to forgive yourself for killing your best friend in the whole wide world, huh?" Larry asked with a caring tone and a snarling grin.

Regina looked at her brother wondering how he did that. How could he be the brother she loved when he was so evil? How did he make his voice sound like the opposite of what his eyes and the rest of his face said? And then she had noticed them, little purple wings dancing over his head.

"Oh, she lightly exclaimed. They're so beautiful. So delicate."

And for the first time in her life, she thought she saw fear in Larry's face. He swatted at the butterflies trying to kill them or at least to get them away from his face.

They fluttered over to Regina and danced about her head. One of them landed on her shoulder and remained there. At first Larry had only noticed that they were no longer bothering him and he turned to Regina to get another dig in when he saw where the Great Purple Hairstreaks had gone. All of a sudden Larry didn't feel much like tormenting his sister. He just wanted to get away from those damn bugs. He didn't understand why it made him so uneasy that they were hanging around Regina like that; he only knew that it did. In fact, he was getting down right uncomfortable.

Regina noticed the change in her brother as they walked side by side. Anyone passing by would have had no idea that she was scared to be near him and he was scared of the butterflies that floated over her head. Regina noticed something else about her brother that was odd that day. Every time they walked past a dog, the dog would seem to brace itself rock steady and let out a low growl. She had never seen these dogs act

Wicked Dreams

like that before. And she knew these dogs. Everyone knew all of the dogs in town. And this was the meeting ground for all of the dog lovers. Everyone romped in the park and had a grand old time. That is, until Larry walked past.

They were approaching old Mr. Carver who was sitting on a bench with his newfound four-legged friend lying on the ground next to him. Regina never let herself believe that Larry had been the one who had killed Mr. Carver's last dog. But today she was beginning to wonder if maybe it was a true story. She loved Mr. Carver's new dog and he was wagging his tail as she walked up to give him a pat on the head. But all of a sudden, the dog began to growl. Regina wasn't afraid because she could tell he wasn't even looking at her when he growled. But it made her feel eerie when she saw that he was looking at Larry who had stopped at the water fountain to get a drink and had just caught up with her.

"Hello, Ginny. Fine day it is. Fine day." Mr. Carver spoke to Regina, ignoring the fact that her brother stood right next to her.

"Same to you, 'ya old fart!" Larry sneered as the two walked on.

Regina awoke from her daydream and took another bite of her sandwich. She looked at her watch. *Time to go back to work already? Did I fall asleep or something?* Regina stuffed her napkin and bread crust into her brown paper bag, stood up and headed back to the accounting office where she had been working for the last five years. She never noticed the dancing wings that followed close behind her or the tails that wagged as she walked back through the park and on to Keppler and Keppler.

Although Regina had just been thinking about her brother, she was still startled when she picked up the phone to find him on the other end.

"Keppler and Keppler. This is Regina."

"Hey, Little Sister Tutu."

Regina cringed. It wasn't just that hearing her brother's voice sent chills up her spine. It was also how deeply it hurt when he called her that name. It made her think of ballet and how her heart still ached to dance. But worst of all, it made her think of Betsy. Poor, poor Betsy. *Oh, if I'd only…*

"Are you there?"

"Yes, I'm here. What do you want?"

"Well, ain't that a fine greeting. Okay, okay, yeah, there's something I want."

"Well, what is it, Larry? Just tell me what you want."

"Well, you see I'm gonna go on this trip, you see, and I need you to come around to take care of the old homestead, you know."

"Take care of it? You wanted it when Mom and Dad died. You've got it. It's yours. You take care of it." Regina couldn't believe these words were coming from her own mouth. She knew if Larry was standing right in front of her, she would not be speaking to him this way. She felt strange to have this kind of courage. *It must be because I haven't seen him for so long. I must have forgotten how scary he can be.*

"Whoa, Little Sister! You sure have changed. Well, if you want to know the truth, there are a few plants that need watering and feeding. But mostly I just want my damn nosy neighbors to see you comin' around so they don't think the place is abandoned and send the old sheriff in. I don't want no one in my house that don't live there."

"Well, I don't live there."

"You know what I mean. I don't ask for many favors from you, Little Sister Tutu, but you know what happens if you don't..."

"I'll do it! I'll do it!" Regina screamed in the phone unaware that her boss was standing in the doorway. She slammed down the phone and began to sob. She felt a hand on her shoulder and looked up to see Mr. Keppler looking down at her. His eyes were watery and his face looked worried.

"Regina, are you okay?"

"Yes, Mr. Keppler. I'm sorry. I don't usually do this."

"I know. That's the first time I've ever seen anyone get a rise out of you. I'm glad to see it, but ... uhh... hoping it wasn't a client."

"No, no, it wasn't a client. It was my brother."

"Your brother? Oh, my Gawd, I forgot who your brother was."

"It's okay. I try to forget too."

"Are you going to be okay? Do you need me to call security or the police or anyone else?"

"No, I'm fine."

"I know it's none of my business, but what did that bastard want?"

"Oh, Mr. Keppler!" Regina was shocked to hear such a word come from Mr. Keppler's mouth. He was an elderly gentleman, a gentleman indeed. He was always professional and always so proper.

"Oh...uh...err... please forgive me Regina. I just never liked your brother. He's evil and foul. I know I shouldn't say that to you. You're his sister. But it is how I feel."

"Mr. Keppler, I couldn't agree with you more. I guess I thought I had put him away with my past. I guess I really thought I'd never hear from him again. He wants me to look after the house while he goes on vacation."

"Are you going to do it?"

"Yeah, I think I will. I am afraid to not do it for him. I'm not sure what the consequences would be. But, you know what? I'm actually looking forward to it. I think it would be good to get to go back in the house where I grew up. There's some pictures of Mom and Dad there that I want. Larry said I could have them. I just never wanted to go in that house when he was there."

"When will you go over?"

"Oh, Gawd, I forgot to ask." Regina answered looking up into the kind and gentle face of old Mr. Keppler.

"Well, listen, if you want to call him back now, I'll wait right here with you to keep you company."

"Oh, thank you so much, but I'm okay. I really can do this," Regina answered as she picked up the receiver.

"Okay, Regina, but you promise to let me know if there is anything I can do for you. Okay?"

"Yes, Mr. Keppler. And thank you for being so thoughtful."

As Mr. Keppler walked out of her office, Regina began to dial the phone number she had memorized so many years ago to recite in her kindergarten class for Ms. Davis. She again was caught off guard by the sense of strength she felt. She gazed out the window while the phone rang and was ready to hear his voice again. Something caught her eye and she realized that there was a small cluster of purple butterflies floating just outside her window.

"Yeah?" Larry's voice came on the other end.

"Larry, it's me, Regina. I forgot to ask when you leave for your trip."

"Poor, dumb Little Sister. I wondered when you'd call me back. I'm leaving tomorrow."

"Tomorrow?"

"Yeah, tomorrow." There was a long pause and then Larry finally spoke again. "You can do it, can't you?"

Regina was surprised to hear a shadow of doubt in Larry's voice. She had never seen any sign of this side of him before.

"Huh? Can you?"

"Yes, I'll stop by tomorrow. Uh, Larry?"

"What?"

"How long will you be gone?"

"Jeezusss! I ain't asking for much!"

"No, it's not that. I was just wondering if I could stay at the house while you were gone. I'd like to, you know, look for those pictures and that other stuff you said I could have."

"Oh, afraid to come by when big brother is home, eh?"

"No, it's not like that."

Amy J. Cooper

"Yeah, I don't care. I'll be gone about a week. Just make sure your butt is out of there by next Sunday. Got it?"

"Yeah, I got it. Thanks, Larry. By the way, you didn't say where you were going."

"Some cabin place out near Hancock. Heard there was good hunting there."

"Hunting? I didn't know it was hunting season."

"Poor, little, dumb sister. Yeah, it's hunting season. For some game, it's hunting season all right."

Regina wasn't exactly sure why Larry's last sentence made her shiver, but it did. It really did.

"Okay, I'll be there tomorrow Larry."

"All right. You better be." And then the phone line went dead.

After spending the rest of the afternoon working on some spreadsheets, Regina was ready for 5:00. She felt exhausted and was anxious to go home, take a hot bath and curl up with a good book. As she headed out of the office, Katrina, the firm's receptionist, called out to her.

"Regina, have a nice weekend!"

"Thanks, Katrina. Is it really Friday? I guess I didn't realize."

"Oh, Regina, you need a life!" Katrina giggled back.

"You may be right. Yeah, you may be right..."

When Regina arrived home, she followed through with her plans. A hot bath drawing, she poured a glass of blush wine and made a plate of cheese and crackers. She grabbed her book and headed to the bathroom. Once in the tub full of bubbles the scent of hyacinth, she sipped her wine and nibbled on her dinner. She didn't notice the book left lying on the rug beside the footed tub. Her thoughts were so preoccupied that she forgot she had wanted to read. She was anxious and she wasn't sure why. Maybe it had something to do with going back to the house tomorrow. But that didn't make much sense to her. The only reason she would be afraid to go back there would be because of her brother, and she knew Larry would not be there. Still, there was something. There was something just out of her reach, something making her feel anxious, excited and afraid all at the same time.

Regina wasn't quite sure how long she had been in the tub when her thoughts brought her back to reality. She awoke to discover the water had grown cold and her fingers and toes had turned into prunes. She stepped out of the tub, dried herself and put her robe on. After putting her dishes away, she climbed into bed. She dreamed that night, but they were not like dreams she had ever had before. She found herself in the woods and she was running. There was something really bad in the woods too, but she wasn't as scared as she thought she should be. She felt strong. She was running as hard as she could, leaping over branches and rocks. She didn't know how graceful she looked as she leaped over the obstacles in the path. She didn't know that this was a ballet dance of sorts. She only knew she had to catch up with the others. They needed her and she would be there for them.

When Regina awoke in the morning, she felt rested, but sore. I must have been running in my sleep, she mused, not realizing the truth of which she spoke. She dressed in jeans and a light sweater and began gathering the things that she wanted to take to her brother's home with her. She found her book on the bathroom floor where she had left it the night before. It was a book about Greek and Roman goddesses.

"Okay, Diana, Goddess of the Woods, let's go!"

It had taken Regina awhile to pack her suitcases and to run a few errands. She was excited about being back in the home she grew up in, yet she purposely took extra time to get there. She really didn't want to run into Larry if she could help it.

When she pulled up into the driveway, she was relieved to see that Larry was gone. His silver car was missing. Well, calling it silver was being nice. It was flat grey with lots of patches of body putty on it. It was loud and smelled bad. And Regina was glad to see it was missing.

She carted her suitcases up to her old room. Even though it really hadn't changed much and still felt like home, Regina unzipped the suitcases and left them out on the floor. She wasn't quite willing to unpack. She went back downstairs and put away the groceries she had picked up on her way over. She had no desire to eat any of Larry's food. When she finished putting away her food, she noticed a note on the table from Larry. She picked it up and read it out loud, "Don't forget to water and feed my plants! Don't forget!"

And feed? Regina's mind went back to the phone conversation she had with Larry yesterday. *Yeah, he did say something about feed the plants.*

Regina was curious so she cautiously walked out to the screened-in back porch to see just what kind of plants would need "feeding." And there they were. There were 6 of them and they were each about 6 inches high. Instead of flowers at the end of their stems, Regina saw what looked like mouths. *Oh, man, leave it to Larry to have Venus Flytraps.*

There on the floor in front of the plant stand was a cooler with a piece of notebook paper taped to it. Regina recognized Larry's handwriting in black marker, "plant food." She pushed back the lid of the cooler and stared in horror at what was held within. It was some sort of meat, but nothing like what she had ever seen in the grocery store before. She didn't want to know. Trying to hold back the impulse to vomit, Regina carried the cooler out to the big garbage can that was resting on the street curb. *Thank God tomorrow is trash day! Thank God!*

"Oh, Regina, it is so nice to see you, Honey."

Regina looked up to see Mr. Carver sitting on a rocker on his front porch.

"Are you visiting, Larry?" He asked, not able to hide the concern in his voice.

"Oh, Gawd no! Larry went on vacation and I'm just going to stay here while he's gone."

"Regina, I'm glad. I was worried..."

"Mr. Carver, you don't have to worry about it. I'm not like him and I certainly don't spend any time with him." Regina walked up to the porch steps to talk to her old neighbor.

"Regina, Honey, why don't you come by tomorrow morning and we'll have some coffee and get reacquainted. I know Bruce would love to have 'ya."

Hearing his name, the black lab's ears perked and his tail began to wag. Regina bent down to rub on his head and he rolled over so she could rub his belly too. She laughed and gave the dog's stomach a good rubbing.

"Well, I've got to go, Mr. Carver. There's some old pictures and stuff I've been anxious to get my hands on."

"Well, bring a few of those with you when you come over tomorrow morning. How's 8:00 sound?"

"Great. I'll be there. Should I bring anything else?"

"Nope. Mrs. Jonathon just dropped off one of her famous apple pies and we'll have that with coffee."

"Oh, yummy! I forgot about Mrs. Jonathon's apple pies! I'll see you then!"

Off Regina went to go search for the pictures and other memorabilia she had longed for. The old man watched her go, knowing he would sleep well with such an angel in the house next door. Nights were not for sleeping when that Larry fellow was around.

Regina started in her parents' old bedroom. She pulled out boxes from under the bed and began to go through them. There were pictures that she had drawn back in elementary school all the way through junior high. There wouldn't be any after that. She stopped drawing after Betsy died. There was a bunch of her old poetry too. Regina read some of them while laughing out loud until she got to the ones she wrote after Betsy died. It was too hard to look at them, let alone read them. The light was getting dim anyway. Regina reached up to the end table next to what had been her father's side of the bed and turned on the lamp. Her eyes dropped down to the clock that was still plugged in after all of these years. *Is it really that late? I better get something to eat.*

Regina went downstairs to the kitchen that held so many fond memories for her. She began to cut up some vegetables to make a big salad and poured a glass of

Wicked Dreams

White Zinfandel. When her meal was prepared, she settled down at the table with her book and began to read the chapter of Diana the Huntress again.

When Regina finished her dinner, she climbed upstairs and went back into her parents' bedroom. *Guess I better put these boxes away. There's nothing else here I want to take back with me.* With that thought, Regina suddenly realized what had been nagging at the back of her mind. There were no boxes of pictures that Larry had drawn. It wasn't so much that Regina wanted to see those pictures, it was more that she was curious that they weren't there. Regina's mother had always been so careful to include Larry in everything. She had always made a big deal about Larry's pictures. He always used dark crayons. And although his pictures were abstract, they clearly appeared to depict blood and death. As horrid as those pictures were, their mother didn't want Larry to feel that they weren't just as important as Regina's pictures of flowers and trees.

Regina turned around and headed down the hall to her brother's room. She did find it a bit odd that he never moved into the master bedroom once he had the house to himself, but then she was staying in her old room. *So what does that mean?* She opened the door and looked into a room that looked as though a hurricane had just blown through it. G*eez!* She glanced around the room and saw a box sticking out from under the bed. She knelt down by the bed and pulled the box out. When she opened it, she saw the pictures he had drawn when he was a kid. But there were others that weren't on yellowed paper. The signature on them was the same as the others, but Regina gasped when she saw that the dates were as recent as last week.

"What in the hell?" Regina dropped the pages back into the box and stood up. She really didn't want to be in that room. Walking out of the room, she noticed another smaller box on the floor in the open closet. It was the jewelry box her father had given her on her 8th Birthday. It had lace and pink valentines on the outside. She knew that when she lifted the lid, there would be a ballerina waiting inside, just waiting for the lid to open and the music to play so that she could dance and twirl. Regina sat on the floor, crossed her legs and picked up the box. She slowly lifted the lid and let out a quiet scream when she realized that Larry had cut off the ballerina's head.

Then she realized that Larry had placed a variety of odd items in the music box. There was a collar, a dog collar. It looked familiar, but Regina couldn't quite remember why. She turned it around in her hands and held the nameplate up toward the light to get a better look at it. *S-p-a-r-k... Oh, my Gawd! He killed Sparky! Oh, my....* Regina ran from the room and just made it to the bathroom in time to vomit into the sink. When she was sure she was done, Regina soaked a wash cloth in cold water and held it to her forehead as she slumped down onto the bathroom rug. She sat there for about an hour, not realizing how much time had passed.

Regina knew she shouldn't have been so surprised to learn that her brother had indeed killed Mr. Carver's old dog, but, still, she had made herself believe for years that was only a horrible rumor. When she felt recovered, Regina held onto the vanity and pulled

Wicked Dreams

herself up. She brushed her teeth, turned out the light and headed back down the hallway towards her brother's room. She needed to know what else was in the box.

Back in her brother's room, Regina dumped the rest of the items from the music box onto the cold hardwood floor. There were all sorts of odds and ends that at one time held great importance to her. There was the little wooden figure that Mr. Carver had whittled for her. It looked like a little wooden man, and she had loved it and carried it with her everywhere for a week and then it had abruptly disappeared. There were pieces of cheap jewelry that she had been given through the years. They weren't worth anything, but Regina had loved them deeply and had been terribly sad when each piece had eventually disappeared. And then there was the ring her mother had given her. Regina cried as she held the sapphire ring in her hand. *What does all of this mean?*

She began to gather up the trinkets and put them back in the lacy box when she realized that she was holding a necklace in her hand. It was a necklace like the one worn around her neck. It was half of a heart. *Oh, God, please, no! Please don't let it be so! Oh, God!* Regina lifted the necklace up to the light and when the pendant stopped spinning, she was staring at the words she had prayed she wouldn't see. Well, they weren't words, not whole words. Regina laid the necklace gently on the wooden floor and slowly took off the one that she had worn around her neck for years. When she laid it on the floor next to the necklace already there, the cryptic inscription was

Amy J. Cooper

completed. She read the words out loud, "RW and BS - Best Friends Forever."

Regina felt the room spinning around her. She could see the blackness filling her vision. She knew she was about to pass out and welcomed it.

Sometime early in the morning, Regina found herself waking up to the feeling of wet sandpaper on her face. Slowly she opened her eyes, which were swollen from crying in her sleep, and looked up into a pair of soft brown eyes.

"Bruce. Oh, Bruce, how did you get in here?"

Bruce could only answer by wagging his tail, but it didn't matter to Regina. She was so glad to have his company. She slowly stood up, her legs and back sore from spending the night on the cold, hard floor. Regina walked down the hallway to the bathroom, pulled her clothes off and climbed into the hot shower. Bruce curled up on the bathroom rug and waited for her to finish.

After she had showered and put on fresh clothes, Regina headed back into Larry's room. Bruce hesitated at the doorway, not willing to step into that room. Regina picked up the small wooden figure, her mother's ring, the collar and Betsy's necklace. These she took with her as she and Bruce went down the stairs and over to the house next door.

The smell of fresh coffee brewing greeted Regina as she stepped up onto the porch and knocked on the screen door. Mr. Carver must have been waiting near the door because he responded to the knock instantaneously.

"Ahh, there you are! I sent Bruce to find you. He's an excellent retriever."

Wicked Dreams

Bruce answered with a moan.

"Uhh... I mean Labrador."

Bruce gave a quick, happy bark and ran into the kitchen where his breakfast waited for him in a big yellow ceramic bowl.

Regina sat at the kitchen table with her old friend and they talked a little while they picked at warmed pieces of apple pie and sipped their coffee.

"Regina, is there something wrong, Dear? You've hardly touched your pie and you sure are being quiet."

"Oh, Mr. Carver, I have something awful to tell you...to show you."

"Well, what is it, Honey? It can't be that bad."

"Oh, yes it is. It's just awful."

"Honey, when you're as old as I am... there isn't anything awful that I haven't heard, seen or tasted."

Slowly, Regina pulled the collar out of her sweater pocket and laid it on the Formica table. "It's Sparky's. I found it in Larry's room. This means that...it means.... Oh, Gawd! If you want me to leave, I'll understand."

The old man stood up and leaned over Regina and held her in his arms. He patted her on the back and softly spoke, "Oh, Honey, I knew that. Don't you see? I always knew that. But you aren't like him. And that will never happen again. Have you seen how Bruce is around that evil brother of yours? It won't happen again. And you weren't to blame anyway. There, there, there." He patted her on the back.

"Mr. Carver, thank you so much. I just couldn't believe it. I guess I always thought that Sparky.... Oh, Mr. Carver, there's something else, something really, really awful."

Amy J. Cooper

Mr. Carver sat back down in his chair and leaned toward Regina, never letting go of her hand. He held it in his and looked deeply into her eyes. "What is it, Honey?"

"Do you remember Betsy Smith? Do you remember my best friend Betsy Smith?"

"Well, sure I do. You two were like peas in a pod. It was such a tragedy what happened to her. Such a shame. Such a ... Oh, you don't mean...not her too?"

Regina carefully laid the newfound necklace on the table and then pulled hers out from under her T-shirt so he could see it. The old man gasped when he read the inscription.

"Oh, Honey, I didn't know. I really hadn't even considered..."

Regina pulled her hand away to wipe the tears from her eyes and blow her nose. The ring on her finger caught the morning sunlight that had sifted in through the kitchen window.

"Isn't that the ring your mother gave you?"

"Yes, I found it there too."

"Oh, I remember that ring. I remember how your heart broke when you lost it. But you didn't lose it, did you? He took it. And he took that poor little girl's life."

Regina began to cry again, sobbing, mourning the death of her friend as though it had happened yesterday. Mr. Carver held her hand and tried to console her until she stopped crying. Then the two sat there in the kitchen in the morning light saying nothing, but yet, saying so much.

After awhile Mr. Carver spoke up. "Regina, do you know where your brother was headed?"

Wicked Dreams

"No, I don't. I didn't really care, so I didn't ask. You don't think he would hurt someone else do you? I mean all of this was done to hurt me. There isn't anyone else I'm close to for him to go after."

"I don't think it matters, Regina. I think once someone can do something like that... I don't know. But I've had this terrible, terrible feeling that something is about to happen. I've been having these dreams..."

"Me too! I'm in the woods and I'm running. There's something bad there, but I'm not scared. I just need to be there to help the others."

"Do you know who the others are?"

"Not really. I just know I need to be there for them."

"That's what I'm talking about Regina. I think your brother is going to hurt someone again. I think he's about to do something really bad, and I think you are the one who can stop him."

"But I don't know where he is."

"Well, put on your detective hat and let's go over that punk's room with a fine tooth comb."

Soon the old man, the young woman and a black lab were seen going into Larry's house. The neighbors who saw this just shook their heads. What did those two think they could possibly do about that evil, evil man?

Up in Larry's room again, Regina found it easier to rifle through his things when she had company. After about an hour, Mr. Carver sat down on the bed and heaved a loud sigh.

"Whew, I need to take a break."

"Can I get you something cold to drink?"

"Well, sure, a nice big glass of.... What is that?"

Amy J. Cooper

"What?"

"That brochure over there on the dresser. It looks like one of those kinds of brochures you get from the travel agent when they're trying to get you to buy a ticket for a Caribbean cruise during hurricane season. Let's take a look at that."

Regina picked up the brochure from the dresser and brought it over to the bed. She sat down next to Mr. Carver and together they looked at the pictures and read the captions.

"Mr. Carver! That's it!" Regina exclaimed when he unfolded the brochure exposing a full spread picture of woods surrounding a log cabin with a large porch and a rocking chair. "That's the place in my dreams."

"That's the place in my dreams too! That must be where you have to go."

Together they read the back of the brochure, "The Meadows. Located near Hancock…"

"I'll go pack."

"I'll go home and fix you up a picnic basket. You'll need your strength."

It didn't take but a few minutes for Regina to pack. After all, she had never really unpacked when she had arrived yesterday. Within a half an hour, she was back at Mr. Carver's house and he was handing her a big picnic basket filled with food to last a week.

"Mr. Carver, you shouldn't have."

"Oh, I had to. It's for you. It's for Betsy. And it's for Sparky." His eyes were turning red and a tear was just about to drop down his cheek.

"I wish you could go with me."

"Me too, Darling, but I'm too old for that stuff."

"I wish Bruce could go."

Wicked Dreams

"I have a feeling you won't need him. I have a feeling you will have lots of friends waiting for you."

"It's just as well. I'll feel better knowing he's here with you. I have a favor to ask. Could you call Mr. Keppler and let him know I'm finally taking that vacation he keeps telling me to take? Tell him all of my current projects are in the top drawer of my filing cabinet."

"Consider it done!"

The two hugged long and hard and then Regina headed out the door. She set the picnic basket on the front passenger seat in case she got hungry on the road, got in the driver's side and then started the car. She had a map taped to her dashboard that she and Mr. Carver had marked her route of travel on. She was headed into the unknown, and although she was afraid, she was actually feeling more confident and brave than she had ever felt before in her life. As she pulled away, she waved at her friends, an old man, a black dog and a fluttering of purple butterflies.

The day went quickly for her and she found she didn't really need the map. She was so driven to reach her destination that she had to work hard to convince herself that she needed to stop at a hotel for the night. It had gotten pretty dark out there in the country, and she knew she should rest and start out the next morning refreshed. She knew she was close and that she would get there early the next day.

She settled into a quiet, clean little motel. After showering, she began to dig into the picnic basket. There was a little cooler with the items that needed to remain cool in it. *Mr. Carver thought of everything!* She snacked on a ham sandwich, some coleslaw and a bottle of lemonade. *Wait, what is that?* Regina

Amy J. Cooper

reached down into the bottom of the basket and pulled out a dog biscuit. Immediately an image of Bruce with a grin on his face and tail wagging flashed through her mind. *Oh, Bruce, thank you too. I may wait to eat it though....* And with that thought in her head, Regina stretched out on the bed and drifted off to sleep. There were no dreams that night, just a good, solid, restful sleep.

In the morning, she nibbled on some goodies from the basket again and had some coffee from Mr. Carver's thermos. Then she was off on the road again. After a few miles, she passed a sign that read "The Meadows, 10 miles ahead."

"You mean I was that close?"

Regina pondered this thought for the next couple miles until she saw something ahead in the road that she couldn't quite identify. It was moving toward her on her side of the road. No, it was a "they." *What?*

Soon she was able to solve the mystery. *They're runners! Way out here? Oh, yeah... I bet they're staying at The Meadows.*

As she was driving past the couple, they were both smiling and the woman waved to her. Regina waved back, but she didn't know why.

"Hey, do you know her?" Paul panted.

"No, I don't. I'm not sure why I waved. I felt like I knew her, though," Dianna answered without much effort. "Hey, you need to take a break?"

"No!..... well, yeah, I do."

"No problem. Let's start walking back to Rose's."

"No problem."

And the two runners turned around and headed back in the direction they had come from, back in the direction the car was headed towards.

*"Lo! Death has reared himself a throne
In a strange city, lying alone
Far down within the dim West,
Where the good and the bad, and the
worst and the best
Have gone to their eternal rest."*

-Edgar Allan Poe (1809-1849)

Chapter 19

When Larry left town, he left hungry. He was so crazy about getting out of there that he had forgotten to eat. A small thing to be sure. For how big of a deal would it be to stop somewhere real quick and get something to eat before he hit the long stretch of country road? No big deal. At least that's what Larry thought. But he had no idea that something would happen at that little restaurant on the outskirts of town that could stand in the way of his long range goal. A big deal and a surprise one at that. And Larry hated surprises.

He pulled into the restaurant parking lot, got out of the car and slammed the door shut behind him.

"She might just fall apart right here if 'yer gonna treat her that way."

Larry turned around to see what fool would have the nerve to talk to him that way. He was surprised to find his old acquaintance, Spike, standing right in front of him. At least he thought it was Spike. He sure didn't look the same, though. His hair was straight, short and clean. He was in a suit too.

Wicked Dreams

"What the hell? Is that you, Spike?"

"Yeah, it's me. How 'ya doin' Larry?"

"I'm okay. What are you doing here?"

"Oh, just taking care of some business."

"Oh, yeah." Larry grinned. "Taking care of business, sure. Speaking of which, are 'ya hungry?"

"Yes, I am. I kind of got here early to tell you the truth and I have some time to kill."

"Well, let's eat together for old time's sake."

"Okay, but not for old time's sake, though. How about for the sake of the future."

"Yeah, I like that," Larry grinned that awful grin of his, and a dog who had been waiting nearby for his master, tucked his tail under his legs and hid behind the bush he was just about to pee on.

The two went into the restaurant not realizing that they were the object of many stares. They did look like an odd pair, a crazy looking big dirty man and a self-proclaimed minister.

But Larry didn't know they were an odd pair. He thought things were just like before. He felt like he had found an old friend who was still just like him. How was he supposed to know that Spike was now some kind of minister? He'd never been to church before.

After they ordered their meals, they began to chat. Larry was so excited he couldn't waste any time. "Spike, I've got another job for you."

"Another what?"

"Another job."

"Oh, no Larry. You don't still live like that, do you?"

"Live like what? What are you saying?"

"Larry, you don't want someone to die, do you?"

"No."

"Oh, thank God! I was afraid that…"

"I want all of them to die. But I'll start with the ones where I'm headed."

"No, Larry! Don't you see? I've seen what it can be like. I've found God. Let me help you. I know I can help you. I'm kind of like a minister now. I'm all they could get up at the prison, but I'm really making a difference…"

Suddenly Larry felt really sick. He knew he was going to throw up but he was in no hurry to find the restroom. He just leaned over the table and looked right into his old friend's eyes. His dinner acquaintance, not realizing what was about to happen, leaned forward as well; but before he could finish his sentence, Larry threw up all over his chest. Some went up into Spike's face, and then it all slid down into his lap.

"That's what I think about what you found!" Larry stood and wiped his mouth off with the back of his hand as he walked out the restaurant door, slamming it shut behind him.

It wasn't so much that the vomit smelled like nothing Spike had ever smelled before, it was the way it burned his skin. He could not clean it off of him fast enough. The waitresses and other diners who had seen what happened all came over to help him. They were all gagging, but all seemed compelled to help him get the wicked stuff off of him.

Larry didn't get hungry again for quite some time. He sat behind the wheel all through the deep of night. He had no map to guide him and he had no need for sleep. He would sleep when he got there. *Oh, and how I'll sleep when it's all over.*

Back at the restaurant, Spike, or Tony as he preferred to be called these days, had a terrible stirring in his belly. He knew something really bad was about to happen, and he knew this would be his chance to make things right. True, he had been headed that way by helping others lately. But there was all that stuff from before, that stuff that no one around here knew about. The killings. *God, please grant me the strength.*

Tony thanked everyone for helping him get cleaned up and he left the restaurant and headed home. He showered and changed clothes, throwing his previous attire into the trashcan. He quickly packed a suitcase and was back in his car within an hour. He wasn't sure exactly where he was headed or even how to get there. But he wasn't worried. He could feel himself being guided in the right direction. He knew what lay ahead was something big and he knew he may never come back this way again, but he gave that little thought. What mattered, what really mattered, was that he stay strong and fight the good fight. *Fight the good fight? What does that mean? Don't think about it, just drive. Drive. Drive. Drive* And drive he did. He didn't want for food or sleep. Like his counterpart, he needed no map to guide him. He drove on automatic pilot, headed to where they would all meet.

*"For memory has painted this a perfect day,
With colors that never fade,
And we find at the end of a perfect day
The soul of a friend we've made."*

- Carrie Jacobs Bond (1862 - 1946)

Chapter 20

Regina checked into The Meadows and quickly unpacked. She loved her little cabin. Although she knew that other cabins were nearby, she felt like she was miles away from any sign of civilization. The cabins had been strategically built in the woods so that visitors would have just this impression.

Regina felt a strange blend of fear and confidence as she stood on the small front porch of her cabin. *Something's about to happen. I can feel it in my bones.* When she slowly turned to get a good look at the woods surrounding her, she felt a stronger sense of confidence. It wasn't just confidence, it was a feeling of safeness. She thought she heard a branch snap and spun around to look in the other direction. And then she felt the sense of fear growing stronger. She had no way of knowing that her fear was not because she had heard a noise, but rather because she was faced in the direction of that which she should fear the most, the evil one. *Calm down. You're acting crazy!*

After several moments, Regina calmed down and realized she was very hungry. She decided to walk into

Wicked Dreams

the nearby town, Hancock, to find somewhere to eat. She planned to also find a market where she could replenish her picnic basket. It looked like rain was coming and she didn't want to be stranded in her cabin without food or something to read. She grabbed her jacket, just in case, closed the cabin door, and headed down the path that would take her to the entrance of The Meadows and to the main road.

As Regina was walking down the dirt road that would take her into Hancock, she kept getting the strangest feeling that she was not alone. She continuously looked over her shoulder, but never to find anyone there. Once, when her gaze flew over the nearby fields of tall grass, she suddenly stopped. Blinking her eyes a few times as tightly as she could, she tried to clear her mind of the vision before her, for it couldn't be real. The image remained the same. There was a pack of dogs of every imaginable and unimaginable breed frolicking about in the tall grass. Over their heads were hundreds of butterflies with wings a rainbow of colors and patterns dancing about in a sort of aerial ballet. Regina recognized some of them from high school biology. There were monarchs, swallowtails and admirals and other types that Regina had never seen before. There was one kind with a dominant presence, some sort of purple-winged one that was the most beautiful of all. What amazed Regina the most was the way that the butterflies seemed to be playing with the dogs. The dogs were barking and jumping at the butterflies while staying just enough away from their delicate wings so as to not harm them. And the butterflies seemed to be chasing the dogs in like manner. It was a song, and the harmony that Regina was witnessing was unlike any song she had ever heard before. She must have stood there for several minutes lost in the strange new world that was playing before her eyes when she was startled by the voice whispering in her left ear.

"I knew you were coming. I knew you were close."

Regina jumped, startled by the sound. She spun around and found herself facing a woman who had the kindest blue eyes she had ever seen. Her face was weathered from years in the sun, and Regina could tell immediately that the woman was younger than she looked. Still, she had an old feel about her... an old familiar feel. For in spite of the fact that the woman had startled Regina, she didn't feel frightened at all. To the contrary, Regina suddenly felt at home. She couldn't stop herself from grabbing the woman and pulling her towards her, hugging her like she was a long lost friend. She found herself sobbing uncontrollably and was confused by this since she really had no idea where the outburst of emotion was coming from.

"There, there, Honey. It'll be okay. We're much stronger than him. It will be okay."

"Huh?" Regina backed away a little, searching her jacket pockets for a tissue so she could blow her nose.

"Well, there's more coming. You got here a little earlier than I thought you would. But don't worry, there's lots more coming."

"Lots more?"

"Yes, Honey, lots more."

"Lots more what?"

"Dogs, Honey. The dogs. Oh, dear. I've been so busy getting ready for you that I forgot you wouldn't know. I forgot I was the one who was supposed to show you. I plum forgot. Now, isn't that funny. I've been so busy doing my job I forgot what it was."

"Your job?"

"Yeah, I'm here to help you. I'm the one that talks to the dogs."

And that was how Regina met Maggie.

*"I dream in my dream all the dreams of the other dreamers,
And I become the other dreamers."*

- *Walt Whitman (1819-1892)*

Chapter 21

Paul and Dianna had raced back to the cabins, showered, and were headed down to Rose's Diner. They were lost in talk as they walked down the wooded path absentmindedly stepping over tree roots that jutted up through the path's surface. Sam and Emily would run ahead, and run back as if to hurry them along. It hadn't taken them long to figure out they were headed to that place where humans ate a lot of food that smelled heavy. That meant they would get all sorts of delicious bites of different kinds of tastes, and they would each get a big bowl of milk.

"You seem worried."

"I know. I just have the strangest feeling. It's like in my dreams, but that usually happens at night."

"Yeah, I usually dream at night too."

"Not that," Dianna playfully hit Paul on the back. "I mean that this feels like I do in my dreams, when I feel like there is someone in the woods with me. But what's different is that when I dream it, it's night time. It's still pretty light out now."

"What kinds of dreams?" Paul asked getting a little more serious.

Wicked Dreams

"Oh, you know, running through the woods, chasing something..."

"With Emily?"

"Well, yes, with Emily. And then...oh, my gawd! You are there too! Why didn't I remember that until now? Paul, you have been in my dreams!"

"Uh, Dianna," Paul spoke as he stopped walking, grabbing ahold of Dianna's arm. "I have been having the same dreams. It's like we are chasing something together, something evil... or are we running away? I'm more scared than I've ever been in my life and then I realize you and Emily are there and I'm not so scared."

"Paul, these dreams..."

"Wait! I have to tell you something. I've been having these dreams for a long time, but they haven't always been in the woods. At first, we were in this meadow and there was something bad there, I mean really bad. This thing, whatever it was, was so bad it was like I could even smell it. And the smell was so bad, I'd wake up sometimes gagging from it."

"That's what I was going to tell you, Paul. I've been having dreams about you for a long time too. But the meadow, or the field, wherever it was, there were these butterflies..."

"The Great Purple Hairstreak!"

"Huh?"

"It's a butterfly...Look, were there purple-winged butterflies in your dreams"

"Yeah, but there were all sorts of other colors too. And there was something about the butterflies. Something would happen to me. I would change somehow."

Amy J. Cooper

"You knew you could do it!"

"Do what?"

"Anything. You could do whatever it was going to take. You knew you could win. You found this strength you didn't know you had!"

"Yes! That's it! Yea, though I walk through the valley of the shadow of death…"

"I shall fear no evil."

Somehow the two had resumed walking while they had been talking and now they stopped at the clearing where the path emptied into the meadow. They stopped and they stared into each others eyes not sure if they should be happy or frightened about their revelation. They only stood silent for a moment when they realized they were not alone. There were wings in flight, dancing gracefully over the tops of the tall meadow grasses.

Having dreamt it before, they both knew what would come next. They reached for each other and held hands so tightly their knuckles quickly turned white. And then it came. The smell. The bad, evil smell overcame their senses. Nothing else existed but that smell. Although they were clinging to each other, neither one felt the same fear they had in their dreams. True, the butterflies seemed to take away most of the fear in their dreams, but this time there was almost none. Maybe it was because this time they were awake. Maybe it was because this time they were standing right next to each other. Or maybe this time it was because of the dogs.

Paul and Dianna looked about 50 yards ahead in the meadow and couldn't believe their eyes. Slowly,

Wicked Dreams

one by one, dog after dog stood up, seeming to just awaken from sleep.

"Gawd, there must be at least 20 dogs out there!"

"28," a voice spoke from behind them.

And that was how Paul, Dianna, Emily and Sam met Regina and 28 of her new friends.

*"...But all the story of the night told over,
And all their minds transfigur'd so together..."*

- William Shakespeare (1564-1616)

Chapter 22

Regina had dinner that night at Rose's Diner with Dianna and Paul. The conversation was long, strange and wonderful. It was like they were old friends who hadn't seen each other for quite some years and needed to catch up. It was also like they were newfound friends and they had so much to learn about each other. And it was wonderful because it filled that empty space, that missing piece of the puzzle that had been growing in all of their minds. Somehow they had all known that they had come to Hancock for a special purpose, and now they felt closer to knowing what it would be.

When the threesome finished dinner, they walked back down the road toward The Meadows. They stopped at Paul's cabin to get Sam and headed over to Dianna's cabin. When they arrived at her cabin, Emily almost knocked them over rushing out the door to see her friend, Sam. While the two dogs romped in the grass in front of the cabin, Dianna and Regina built a campfire and Paul poured some white wine.

Before long, the two-legged creatures were wrapped in blankets and huddled in lawn chairs, and the four-legged creatures were cuddled up on the soft earth, all in front of the comforting fire as a melody of words intertwined with the smoke and drifted up into the dark night sky. The conversation had been light and calm, but eventually the words turned to those that they all knew must be spoken, words about the present, words about the very near future, words that raised the hair on their arms.

"I came here to find my brother. I just found out that he'd done these horrible, horrible things and.... Well, it's not like I thought about what I would do when I found him. I just knew I needed to get to him as fast as I could," Regina spoke softly wrapping the blanket tighter around her shoulders.

"What kind of things did he do?" Paul asked.

"He killed my best friend!" Regina could barely blurt out as the tears welled in her eyes.

"Oh, my gawd! Are you okay, Honey? How? When?" Dianna's words rushed out in a flurry as she moved her chair closer to Regina's and put her arm around her shoulders, trying to comfort her.

"Oh, it was a long time ago. I went through all kinds of therapy after it happened. I've learned to deal with it. It's just that... well, I knew Larry was bad. I've always been afraid of him. I just had no idea that he could do something like that."

"Do you want to talk about it?" Dianna asked as she gently rubbed Regina's back.

"Yeah, I know now that you guys have to know. It's really important that you know." And Regina began her story.

"You see, I was still a kid and my best friend and I had stayed late at class that night. Ballet class. We'd studied for years together. I was auditioning for scholarships so I could keep studying, so I could really dance, you know? Well, this one night, like I said, we stayed late. Betsy took our stuff down to the car and I was still upstairs talking to this man... this man that was going to get me a scholarship so I could study in New York. Betsy came up once to ask if I was coming and I brushed her off. Oh, gawd, it still makes me sick to think about it. I told her to go wait for me and that I'd be right down. I can still see the look on her face. I must have sounded really mean. I remember that Betsy went back downstairs and after a couple minutes, the man I was talking to... I can't remember his name. Anyway, he got in this real hurry and flew out of there. I thought that was weird and I ran downstairs to tell Betsy about it, but when I got to the car, she was... she was..." Regina's voice broke off into heavy sobs.

"There, there, Regina. You poor thing." Dianna tried to console her new friend.

After a few minutes Regina caught her breath, dried her eyes, and was ready to go on. "There's more I have to tell you.

"I found this out the other night when I went back home. Larry had asked me... no, that's wrong. Larry told me I would look after the house while he went on vacation. He never goes on vacation. But I always do what he tells me to because...well, because I'm so damn afraid of him. Anyway, it's the house we grew up in and I really wanted to go because there's some stuff there I've been wanting, but I never wanted to go over when Larry was there.

Wicked Dreams

"So the other night, I was there. I was home and it kind of felt good. I started going through boxes of stuff looking for these pictures I wanted of my mom and dad. They died several years ago, and I wanted these pictures... Well, anyway, I was looking through all of this stuff and I found this old jewelry box of mine. I'd lost it when I was a kid and I remember how much I cried because my dad had given it to me. So I found this box and what was inside just about killed me. I found stuff that made me realize that Larry had killed Betsy and also Mr. Carver's dog, Sparky."

"Who's Mr. Carver?"

"He's my old neighbor. He still lives next to Larry. He's such a nice old man. Everyone, including Mr. Carver, always said that Larry had killed Sparky. And I guess I always knew he was capable of it, but I just couldn't let myself believe it was true. How could my own brother be a murderer?"

"What did you find that made you know it was Larry that did it?" Paul asked.

"I found Sparky's collar. It was Larry. I know it." Regina reached in her pocket as she spoke and pulled out the small wooden figure that she had found in her old jewelry box that night.

"What's that?" Paul asked noticing the small figure in her hands.

"It's just this little wooden man that Mr. Carver made for me when I was a kid. Larry always hated it. I think he was jealous." Regina handed the wooden piece over to Paul.

"Hey, look, Dianna. It looks like Fred from down at Rose's Diner." Paul handed the piece to Dianna.

"No, I don't think so. But he does look familiar. He looks like... he looks like...oh, my gawd! I know who he looks like! The man in my dream! That's the man in my dream!"

"What dream?" Regina and Paul asked together.

"The other morning ... you know when you are almost awake, but not quite and so you're not sure if what you're seeing is real or if it's in your dreams? Well, I was in that place in my head when I had this weird dream and I thought there was this man in my cabin. He was kind of hiding in the corner of my room."

"What did he look like?" Regina asked.

"Well, he was big, kind of sloppy big and kind of strong big. He had black curly hair, I think. It was hard to see him. He was like a shadow. But I do remember that he smelled bad."

"Why would you think of him? My little wooden man doesn't look anything like that. He doesn't really have a face, and he certainly doesn't look like he has any hair."

"But he does, Regina. Just look at him." Dianna handed the little man back to Regina.

"Oh my gawd! It's him! It's Larry! How can that be? It never looked like Larry before? What's happened? What's going on?"

The urgency in Regina's voice startled the sleeping dogs from their warm nap. Emily jumped up and ran over to Regina, almost jumping on her lap so that she could sniff the small wooden figure in her hand. She immediately jumped back down and tilted her head back and let out a long and haunting howl. By this time Sam had already run over to see what his friend had discovered and soon he had joined in the song of the night, the song of the moon, the song to unite the pack that had been growing in the nearby meadow. And the group that had just become 40 strong joined in the harmony. Soon there was a sound like no other heard before, and the three humans could only stare at each other and try to stay warm as the chill traveled up and down their spines.

The aria eventually faded into the distance, but the threesome still sat in silence, unable to speak, unable to react to the strange entity they had just witnessed. They were startled from the soundlessness by a voice coming from the woods.

"What the heck was that?" Tony asked as he stepped up to his neighbors' campfire.

And that was how Tony, formerly known as Spike, met the newly formed clique that had gathered around the fire that night to learn of each other and begin to prepare for what was soon to be.

*"The poor dog, in life the firmest friend,
The first to welcome, foremost to
defend."*

*- George Noel Gordon, Lord Byron
(1788-1824)*

Chapter 23

The next morning, Regina awoke early. She slipped into the jeans and sweatshirt she had worn the night before. They still smelled like the campfire. She sat on the old rocker on her front porch and sipped on the coffee from Mr. Carver's thermos that Rose had filled the evening before. Staring out over the dewy grass and into the woods that outlined her cabin, it was hard to imagine the frightening way she felt the night before. She could hear the birds singing from the trees and could even see them flitting about from branch to branch. There were butterflies too. The bouquet of colors seemed unending as they danced in an aerial ballet. Seeing the butterflies made it even harder for Regina to get that scared feeling back that she had the night before. She found herself feeling stronger and stronger as she gazed at the dancing wings. In fact, she was feeling down right undefeatable. *Undefeatable?*

Slowly she stopped rocking, stretched out her arms and legs and let out a long yawn. *Guess I'll head on down to Rose's. Those guys will be there pretty soon.*

As Regina walked, she thought about Paul and Dianna. She was looking forward to seeing them again.

Wicked Dreams

They had agreed that after their morning run, they would meet Regina and Tony at Rose's for breakfast. Then they would all go together to Maggie's. For some reason, it was very important to Regina that the others meet Maggie. Maybe it was because Maggie would be the one to help put the pieces of the puzzle together. She knew that something was about to happen and that Maggie was somehow a part of it, even if only as a source of grounding, a source for answers, and the one who understood the dogs.

Regina headed down the path that lead to the meadow and on to the road. As she wandered along, she hardly realized that her feet were somehow stepping over the roots that protruded through the earthen path and over and around fallen branches. Her thoughts were lost in the memory of last night's conversation. She was trying to understand what it was that bothered her about Tony. Although Tony had only joined them for a short while last night, there was something about him that had left a lasting impression. Regina knew that he was some kind of minister, but there was something else about him that she couldn't quite grasp. She wasn't quite afraid of him, and yet she felt something foreboding whenever his face would float before the eye of her memory. *Maybe Maggie will know the answer to this one too.*

Soon, Regina was to the clearing. Just as she stepped out of the woods, she was greeted by her two new friends. They were out of breath, wet with sweat and slightly smelly. They all laughed as they nearly knocked each other down.

"I thought you guys would already be down at Rose's!"

Amy J. Cooper

"Well, we got a late start. And Pokey here is just learning how to breathe while he runs," Dianna laughed.

"Hey! Whaddy a expect when your breathing teacher is an asthmatic!" Paul responded in like manner.

"We'll shower and be down at the diner in no time," Dianna said.

"Okay. I'll see 'ya down there," Regina responded. Now she couldn't stop laughing either. *What is it about these guys that makes me feel so good?*

After a moment they parted ways. Dianna and Paul off running down the path toward the cabins, and Regina walking through the long grass of the field and down to the road. When she reached the diner, she found the regulars were all there. She sat down on one of the white plastic chairs that were placed out front of the diner for mornings just like this. The sky was fairly clear, but the few puffy clouds and the slight coolness in the air hinted that a storm was still on its way. As she sat down, she heard the door of the diner open and turned around expecting to see Rose stepping out. Instead she found herself looking into Tony's eyes. *What is it about him that makes me feel so uneasy?*

"Hi! I was afraid you guys weren't coming."

"Yeah, I just saw Dianna and Paul. They'll be here in a minute or so," Regina answered. She struggled to pull off her sweatshirt, warm from her morning walk.

"Here, let me help you." Tony suddenly stopped in mid-movement. His eyes stared in horror at the gold necklace that hung on Regina's neck.

"What is it, Tony? Are you okay?"

Wicked Dreams

"Uh, yeah. I mean, no, I'm not. I mean… oh, gawd. Now I know why I know you. Oh, Regina, I have something terrible to tell you…"

But Tony was interrupted by the rumbling sound of the Harley Sportster as it pulled up in front of the diner. And even though the engine was quickly shut off, the level of noise didn't dissipate because the two riders were making just as much noise as the pipes did. The folks who were in the diner came out to see what the ruckus was all about. They instantly broke out in laughter, clapping their hands. But no one was laughing louder than Dianna who was sitting on the front of the seat with a white-knuckled Paul clutching her waist. And no one was laughing as softly as Tony. In fact, he wasn't really laughing at all. He couldn't take his eyes off the necklace worn by the young lady who stood by his side.

Tony didn't get a chance then to tell Regina how he knew who she was. Once he saw the necklace, he remembered the picture of Regina that Larry West had shown him all those years ago. He needed to know which young girl was the sister and which was the friend so he would get the job done right. At the time his thinking had been that there was nothing worse than a pissed-off client to ruin business. But today he was a different man. And today, when those thoughts came rushing back to him, he spun around, knocked his chair over and ran to the men's room to throw up.

Tony was in the bathroom for quite awhile. If anyone had walked in on him, they would have found him on his knees. He was no longer embracing the porcelain, as some would say, but instead was holding his hands open, palm side up, looking toward the ceiling and lost in prayer. His face which had grown rigid, stricken with the pain from the memory of someone he used to be, was beginning to soften. Eventually he actually looked somewhat serene.

When Tony returned to the table, the others were in mid-discussion, but the talking stopped as soon as they saw him.

"Are you okay, man?" Paul asked.

"Yeah. I'm okay now. Thanks. Not too hungry though."

"Are you sure?" Regina inquired.

"Yeah, I'm real sure."

Dianna chimed in, "Well, if you're up to it, then, Regina was about to take us to meet Maggie."

"Okay. I'm ready."

After paying their checks, the four headed up into town. Maggie lived just on the other side of "downtown." The four marveled how you could take what seemed like one step out of town and you would already feel like you were in the country.

When they approached Maggie's front yard, Emily and Sam ran ahead barking and leaping into the air. The sounds of barking greeted them. Paul and Dianna rounded the corner of the house first and they stopped in their tracks when they saw what lay before them. There had to be 50 dogs or more behind Maggie's house. There was room for them, to be sure, since Maggie owned about 30 acres. It wasn't that they were all behind her house, it was that there were so many and it was what they were doing. They were all standing about in what looked like mini-group discussions. It truly looked like some sort of party, and Paul and Dianna definitely felt like they were the party crashers.

Wicked Dreams

Tony and Regina didn't realize the others had stopped and they tripped into them as they came around the corner. The sound this made changed the scene before them. The dogs all stopped their "conversations" and all turned to face their two-legged guests.

"Oh, there you are!" Maggie stepped out her back door and down the porch steps toward them. "I was hoping you'd get here soon." She gestured toward the circle of old wooden chairs near her flower garden. "Please sit down. We haven't much time, and we have a lot to talk about."

She was a pleasant looking woman. And although her clothes were old and worn, you could see that the dirt on her skirt was from hard work. There were other skirts like it hung on the line to dry. They looked the same, but they were stiff and clean. She had those kind of blue eyes that you felt you could see through. Her face was aged, but it seemed more from the sun than from years. True she was older, but not as old as she looked. The others quickly discerned this as they watched her pour five glasses of lemonade and set the pitcher on the table near the chairs.

Soon they were all held captive by the sound of Maggie's voice. Some of the story that the old woman told matched what Regina had told them the night before. But no one wanted to interrupt to let Maggie know that. It was as though they needed to hear it again. But then, some of it was new too. They understood that they had all gathered for the same reason. Something was about to happen and whatever it was, it was going to take all of them to win. They were on the good side, so they had that in their favor. But it was the bad side that confused them. It was difficult to maintain a sense of confidence when they weren't quite sure who the enemy was. But they were about to find that out.

"Regina, Honey, listen closely to what I am about to tell you. You are surrounded by a circle of friends who will stay by your side. You are protected by their goodness and their strength. And right now, I must tell you three things. One is a riddle. But you can only accept the other two if you draw on the strength of your circle of friends.

The first is that the enemy has come in the form of someone close to you. It is your brother."

Regina let out a gasp. She knew that her brother was bad and she knew that she had this unstoppable urge to find him, but she didn't realize that all of this was part of the same. "But..."

"Honey, there was never anything you could do. It had a hold on him a long time ago, long before either of you were even born. Your brother was never really your brother. He has always been this thing that must be defeated. It is an evil thing, a soldier, if you will. It was sent here as a scout. If it sees that good still stands strong, it will be defeated and it will vanish into the darkness until it is called upon again. This is a battle that has been fought before. Long, long ago, two companions came together to fight this battle. The two companions were a man and a dog. They were victorious, as you must be. Because if you lose... But let's not think of that. Let us think about fate. Fate has brought you together now to fight this battle. Those who encircle you and all of these dogs have come from miles away to help you."

Regina was trembling. She was deeply saddened by what she was hearing, and yet she didn't feel surprised. She had always known there was something about Larry. In fact, she had always felt sort of guilty that she couldn't love her brother more, but now she understood why.

"You said there were three things..." Regina managed to say through her muffled sniffs.

"Yes. Now, I want you to trust me. You must believe in what I am about to tell you. You must believe me and trust me. Promise me."

"I promise."

"There is one among your circle of strength that at one time was joined with your enemy. He is no longer a part of that evil world. You must trust and believe that he is now your strongest ally, for there is none so strong on the side of good as one who has seen the horror of the evil world."

"Who is it?" Regina whispered.

"Uh...errr... it's me, Regina. It's me." Tony's face was white as he looked into Regina's face watching for her reaction. It was blank. He knew he needed to say more.

"My name used to be Spike. I didn't know God then. I was the one who was in the car with... with... I was the one who..."

"Betsy!" Regina screamed. "No! No, it was Larry.... It was.....Oh, gawd!"

"Your brother paid me to do it. It was supposed to be... well, it was supposed to be... more messy. But I couldn't do it like he said. I did it so she wouldn't know... so she would pass on before she even knew what was happening to her."

"But, you're supposed to be some kind of minister," Regina whispered.

"I am, and a day never goes by without me regretting my past. I'm doing what I can to make up for it. You've got to believe me. I am so sorry. I am so sorry."

"I don't believe you."

"The necklace you are wearing. There is another half to it. I gave it to your brother."

Regina's face went translucent as she pulled the other necklace from her jacket pocket. She had wanted to wear it, but hadn't been able to bear looking at it again since she found it.

"It was you."

"Yes, it was me. But you must listen to me. I..."

"Why aren't you in prison?"

"They never found enough evidence to arrest me. But now I wish they had. I have been living in hell. Regina, she wasn't the only one, but she was the one that changed me. After her... well, I've never been able to get her face out of my mind. I know I will never be forgiven. But at least now God is giving me a chance to really do something good. You must let me help you."

"No, I can't. I just can't."

Maggie had been sitting silently in her old chair watching and listening. Now, she leaned forward and spoke quietly to Regina. "You said you would trust me. I am telling you that this man is the one you must stay the closest to. This man will save your life. You promised that you would believe me."

Regina stared at Maggie through her red and swollen eyes. "I hardly even know you. Why should I trust you?"

"Oh, Regina, because you know you should. Look deep into your heart. You know that you should trust me. And you know that the man before you was once

Wicked Dreams

a lost soul, but now he is found. You know in the deep of your heart that what I say is true. And you know you have something you can tell this man that will give him the feeling that you can accept him, if even just a little. You know something that can ease his heart just a little. Now tell him."

"But… how could you know? I never told you…"

"I know everything. Now tell him."

"Tony," Regina began, "Betsy was going to die anyway."

"Well, sure, we are all gonna someday," Tony nervously laughed.

"No, that's not it. Betsy had leukemia. She was going to die anyway. You just made it so that she didn't have to go through any more treatments."

"But she was dancing," Tony couldn't believe what he was hearing.

"Yeah, but she was supposed to quit. It was getting too hard for her and she was supposed to quit. And then… and then she didn't have to, because she died."

"Oh, gawd! Just like my sister." And then Tony broke down and cried. He cried long and hard, purging years of pain from his soul. He knew that this news didn't make everything all right. What he had done was still the most vile of sins. But this news made it more bearable. This news gave him the confidence he needed to do what he had come here to do.

"Maggie," Regina finally spoke, "you said there were three things you needed to tell me."

"Yes. The third message is for all of you. It is about power. You need to know that besides what you

Amy J. Cooper

carry inside you, you have the power from three other sources."

"What are they?" they all asked together.

"Well, by now you have probably guessed that one source is your friends here," Maggie spoke as she swept her arm gesturing toward the dogs who were all lying in the grass, facing the circle of chairs with heads cocked and ears up. "And they are lead by Emily and Sam."

"Emily?" Dianna gasped.

As if in answer, Emily looked at Dianna. Even though she could speak no words, the incredulous look on her face said plenty.

"I'm sorry, Girl. I didn't mean it that way." Dianna said bending down to ruffle Emily's ears.

"What are the other sources?" Paul asked.

"Butterflies."

"Butterflies? Yes, of course, the butterflies," Paul responded.

And as if on cue, hundreds of butterflies suddenly appeared and danced over Maggie's garden.

"Yes," said Dianna.

"Of course," Regina added.

And they all sat for several minutes watching the colorful wings of the butterflies as they danced over their heads and then slowly, one by one, drifted away.

"The third one. Maggie, what is the third source?" Regina asked, turning back toward Maggie.

"That is the riddle, Regina. I cannot tell you the third source, but I can tell you that it comes from an object. Something that you have had for a long time, but you didn't know it for years. It is something you have only recently found again," Maggie answered.

"But I don't know what that means, " Regina answered with a hint of panic in her voice.

Maggie patted her hand. "Don't worry Honey. When you need to use it, you'll know."

For the next several hours the circle of friends spoke. Sometimes they sat silently for several moments. The dogs remained facing them as though listening to every word. And somewhere, not very far from them at all, the other side was preparing for what was about to come.

* * * * *

"Will this stuff kill butterflies?" Larry was holding up a gallon can with an attached sprayer on it.

"Now what in the world would you want to kill butterflies for? We ain't got that many here that they could be so much a problem," Fred answered, a little afraid to step too close to the strange man in his shop.

"Well, I do. Now, tell me, will this work?"

"Well, actually the best way, if you really gotta do it, is with fire. But that ain't legal no more so it only happens when there's one of them there natural wild fires."

"Okay, I'll take these gas cans and I want them filled."

"Now, Mister, you can't be setting no fires. That ain't legal and it's just plain crazy with all these trees here and..." Fred's voice cut off when Larry grabbed his wrists and twisted them hard.

"Just get me what I'm asking for and there won't be any trouble. Understand?"

"Yeah, I understand." Fred took the cans out to the pump and filled them. Yeah, he'd give the guy what he wanted and then he'd hotfoot it down to the Sheriff's office as soon as the weirdo was out of his sight.

And Fred did follow through with his plans, but convincing the Sheriff was another matter. Fred ended up leaving the office slamming the door behind him. "It's on your head if something bad happens!" he yelled over his left shoulder as he stormed down the sidewalk toward Rose's Diner.

Meanwhile, Larry had made it back to his cabin. His was on the far end of the property. It was actually a shed where equipment and tools had once been stored. He had moved in without checking in with the office of The Meadows. On his second day there, one of the groundskeepers had stopped him and told him he couldn't stay. *But he won't be yapping his lips to anyone else about it will he?* Larry grinned, his face looking like some sort of bad clown on a late night horror flick.

The awful shadow of some unseen Power
Floats though unseen among us –
visiting
This various world with as inconstant
wing
As summer winds that creep from
flower to flower

- Percy Bysshe Shelley
(1792-1822)

Chapter 24

The scene was much the same as the night before, only there was another chair around the fire. Tony was leaning back with his head tilted toward the night sky. He didn't even realize that his hands were ruffling Sam's fur as Sam looked up at him. Instead his thoughts traveled beyond the storm of stars that lit the sky above. They traveled to the highest place there is, that place that is beyond our existence and yet is within each of us, whether we choose to acknowledge it or not. His heart was heavy and ached as he prayed. It wasn't forgiveness he prayed for. It was strength. He knew that something was about to happen, something beyond his wildest dreams. And he knew that he was brought here to help the others who sat with him around the crackling fire. And he would do that, he would do it to his death. He didn't pray that his life be spared. Instead he prayed that he would not breathe his last breath until all was done. *Thy will be done.*

Amy J. Cooper

Regina mistook Tony's expression and thought he was staring in awe at the millions of stars lighting the dark of night. She looked up as well and exclaimed, "There he is."

"There's who?" Dianna asked.

"Orion."

"Oh, yes. I see him. I always look for the three stars that mark his belt."

"Did you know that he was in love with Diana The Huntress?" Regina asked the group.

"I guess I don't know much about that stuff. But I've always wanted to learn. Guess I just never found the time." The sense of foreboding that fell over the group could be heard in the tone of Paul's voice.

"Orion used to hunt with Diana. They fell in love and were planning to get married when a terrible thing happened. Apollo, Diana's brother, was terribly jealous of them and plotted to somehow end their relationship. One day, Apollo saw Orion wade out into a lake. When he got far enough out that only his head was above the water, Apollo called Diana over for a contest. From the shore it was impossible to see that what was out in the lake was not a log. Apollo challenged his sister to hit the dark thing in the distance. Being the Archer-Goddess, Diana sent out an arrow that pierced the "log" and won the contest. But then the waves brought the body of her lover to shore. She was so overcome with grief that she gathered Orion into her arms and placed him up in the sky.

"If you look there you can see his sword." Regina spoke as she pointed up to the illuminated memorial. "And there is his dog, Sirius."

Wicked Dreams

As though understanding completely, both Sam and Emily looked up at the heavenly dog and they both barked and wagged their tails.

No one in the group said anything. In the short time that they had gathered at The Meadows, they had come to accept that in this new world this kind of behavior made sense. Even if they didn't understand it, they knew that somehow it made sense, so they accepted it.

"But I don't understand..." Regina spoke out loud.

"What ?" Dianna turned toward her new friend.

"The sky."

"Oh, I really don't know that much about stars either."

"No. Not that. We shouldn't be able to see the stars."

"What do you mean?" Now Dianna was leaning so far forward in her chair she nearly tipped it over.

"Remember how cloudy it was. It's been acting like a storm was coming since yesterday. Even when we were building this fire, we were saying we thought the rain would chase us away."

"That's right!" Tony seemed to snap out of his daydream. "I can't even see a cloud anywhere."

"Shhhh. What was that?" Paul jumped out of his chair.

"What?" Now Dianna was on her feet too. "I can't see anything. Where did it sound like it was coming from?"

"I don't know. I couldn't tell."

"I know."

They all turned to look at Regina who was looking down at Sam and Emily. The dogs were standing side by side and staring off into the darkness of the woods, staring in the direction that had been the source of Regina's apprehension earlier that day.

"They're not sure." Regina spoke again.

"Sure of what?" Paul asked, his eyes not leaving Sam's.

"If it's here or not," Regina answered.

"If what's here?" Tony joined in. "I mean, how do you know…"

Regina looked into the faces of each of the others as she explained. "Maggie taught me some things about them, about the dogs. I didn't understand why she was telling me so much. I thought it was just because she's crazy about dogs. But now, after what she told all of us today, I understand the reason.

"When they stand like that with their tails angled down and the ends kind of flipped up, it means that they aren't sure if there is something threatening out there or not. Even the look on their faces says that's what they're thinking. See how their ears are kind of flat out to the sides and their foreheads are all wrinkled? They look like they're about to growl, but not quite. Maggie said that was really important to know."

"What was important to know?" Tony whispered as he moved closer to Regina.

"Maggie said to watch the dogs' faces. She said to not do anything but watch until their faces went from that…" she pointed to their canine companions, "…to a growl. She said their ears would go up and back and they would open their mouths to start to growl. Their tails would go up, but kind of crooked like, not straight. She said it was important to know that because it could happen so subtly that you may not realize it. She said you need to know because as soon as they do that, it means the danger is there and you have to act fast."

"Thanks, Regina. But I'm not finding this information very comforting." Paul moved closer to Dianna.

Regina laughed and the others turned to see that Sam and Emily had snuggled up on the ground near the fire and were deep in sleep.

"Geez! How long were we standing there scaring the crap out of each other?" Paul asked.

"I don't know," Tony responded, "but I'm still feeling a little spooked."

"You guys know there's something going on here." Dianna raised her voice to just above a whisper. "We better remember what Maggie told Regina. It must be something she really thinks we need to know or she wouldn't have made such a big deal of telling her."

The foursome sat back down in their chairs and were silent for several minutes.

"Would you guys object to a sleepover?" Regina finally broke the silence. "I'm just not sure I want to be alone tonight."

"Excellent idea!" Dianna perked up. "I have the biggest cabin. We can stay in mine."

"How do you rate?" Paul asked laughingly.

"Well, I knew I was going to be here for awhile. I came out here to work. So I got a place that I would be able to spread out in. There's a big bed and a couple couches that pull out."

With that decided, they all seemed somewhat relieved and were able to laugh and talk for awhile longer. Eventually they all grew tired and decided it was time to turn in. They left the fire burning as they all walked together to each other's cabins to gather whatever essentials they each needed. When everyone was ready, they smothered the fire with dirt and settled into Dianna's cabin. Dianna and Regina took the big bed, Tony and Paul each took one of the pull out couches and Emily shared her favorite rug with Sam. There was a sense of security having them all in the same room together, and it didn't take long before everyone was fast asleep, lost in dreams.

Somewhere in the night, in that place that isn't quite sleep, isn't quite dreams, and isn't quite reality, somewhere in that lost dimension, the evil thing began to stir. Emily began to lightly kick her feet, back and forth. She seemed to be running in place. She let out little barks. They weren't loud enough to wake the others, not the humans, but Sam heard it. He floated into the dream world to join his friend. They were running side by side when they suddenly stopped and scanned the woods surrounding them. The stars lit the night as if to show them where they were, but they would have known even in the pitch black of night. The sense of scent that a dog has can lead her home even when she is miles from her destination. Emily and Sam closed their eyes, a movement that enhanced their ability to comprehend scents. Then they looked at each other as if to say they knew.

Emily and Sam had traveled in their dreams to just outside Regina's cabin. The smell they were picking up was getting stronger and stronger, and soon there was no doubt that the source was upon them. The evil thing was there. They saw a big shadowy creature slowly move its way up toward the cabin. It reached the porch and then hesitated by the window as though deciding whether or not to go in.

Wicked Dreams

That was when Emily and Sam woke themselves up. They knew that the dreams were about to end. The bad thing in their dreams was now in their real world. They had a job to do and they needed to start now. They both stood and faced the cabin window.

Dianna slept lightly and she always knew when Emily awoke during the night. She opened her eyes. The star-filled sky shed enough light in the room that she could see the twosome facing the window. They seemed to be waiting for something, something that was getting closer.

"What is it, Girl?" Dianna murmured, not wanting to wake the others.

But Emily didn't move. She didn't look back at her master. She remained still.

"What is it?' Paul's voice drifted across the room.

"I'm not sure. But I'm feeling really weird about this." Dianna whispered back.

"I better wake up Tony."

"I'll nudge Regina."

"Don't bother I'm awake," came the voice next to Dianna.

"Me too." Tony coughed lightly as he tried to clear his throat as quietly as possible. "What's going on?"

"I'm not sure," came Dianna's hoarse voice, "but Sam and Emily are on alert."

"I can't see them," Paul whispered.

"Me neither."

"Me neither." Regina's voice filtered softly through the room. "Dianna, can you see them?"

"Yeah."

"What do they look like?'

"They look like they did at the fire. They look like they're almost ready to growl. Their tails are kind of down and curled at the end."

"That means it could be near, whatever it is." Regina gasped.

"Okay. Here's what we should do..." Dianna had no idea where her courage was coming from. "You guys move really slowly and as quietly as you can and work your way to the back door. It might be close enough it can hear or see us. I'll keep an eye on Sam and Emily. When I say 'Now!' you'll know that they did that face and tail thing Regina told us about so you guys run like hell. Got it?"

Dianna heard three affirmative responses and could feel her guests slowly moving toward the back of the cabin. And then she began to move, ever so slowly, never taking her eyes off Emily and Sam. She could feel a slight breeze from the night air that the opened back door let into the cabin. She was slowly moving backwards towards her friends when she noticed a fluttering of movement near the front window. She froze, blinking her eyes trying to focus on the image that played before her. *What am I looking at?* And as soon as she thought the question, she saw the answer. *Butterflies.*

"Guys, are you there, she whispered."

"Yeah, c'mon Dianna." Paul softly answered.

"The butterflies are here," she answered.

"Oh, gawd!" Paul moaned.

"I can see them flying around the front window. I'm trying to see..." Dianna fell silent.

"Dianna? Dianna? What are you doing?"

"NOW!" Dianna screamed.

Wicked Dreams

Suddenly she bolted through the door. Emily and Sam were close behind her. The others had only gotten a few steps ahead of them and together they all ran into the dark of the woods, the dark of the night, the dark of the unknown.

It was like running in a dream. Everything seemed to be moving in slow motion. They ran through the woods, finding their way through the branches and vines. They ran for several minutes until Tony collapsed. Gasping for air, he stumbled to his knees.

"Go!" he wheezed. "Go on without me!"

"No!" Regina grabbed his arm trying to help him to his feet. Paul and Dianna ran back to help.

"Shhhh…something's happening." Paul said under his breath.

Emily and Sam were standing rigid looking off to their right. They heard the sounds of branches breaking and running feet. Lots of them.

"Oh, my gawd!" Regina screamed, although it came out like a moan.

"Wait!" It was Dianna. "Look at Emily and Sam! Look at them! They're wagging their tails."

It was true. The two dogs were standing side by side facing the direction they had all just come from. And their tails were wagging while they were looking into the dark woods. The sound from the woods was getting louder and louder as it came closer and closer. And then they came out from the dark edge of the woods. One by one what looked like about a hundred dogs emerged and stood still, each one staring at the group that was staring at them. Emily and Sam slowly moved up to the one that had emerged first. He seemed to be the leader. They sniffed noses and stood still for a moment. Then he turned to the rest of the pack and about 20 dogs split out and headed in the direction Dianna and the rest had just come from.

"What the…" Paul's voice broke the silence.

"It's a decoy." Dianna answered.

"She's right." Regina agreed. "They're going back so that we can get away."

Tony was standing now. He had caught his breath, but not his courage. And then the other source of their strength was upon them once more. The vision of fluttering wings in the moonlight fell around them. But Paul wasn't aware of the butterflies. He was confused by something else. *How can we have moonlight? Where did the moon come from? It wasn't there earlier.*

As if she could hear his thoughts, Regina answered. "It must be the Huntress Diana. She's also the Goddess of the Moon."

"Where are we?" Tony found his voice.

"Just look up at the stars," Dianna answered. "See Orion? Now, remember, he would have moved some since the fire, so that means we should go …" But before Dianna could finish her sentence she looked up to see the remaining eighty or so dogs headed away from them. They would take a few steps and look back. "They want us to follow them."

Regina answered, "Um-hum. Remember Diana the Huntress didn't go anywhere without her dogs. Let's go."

And then they all ran through the woods somehow finding their way to the path that would take them to the road. As they ran, they could hear in the distance the barking and howling of the dogs that had left them earlier. There were a lot of other noises too. Noises they had never heard before, but noises they knew all the same. It was the sound of evil and the sound of war, the sound of death. It was interrupted by a sharp yelp and then it grew silent for a moment. The group was so sensitive to this interruption that they almost stopped moving. But then they heard the sounds becoming louder and closer again. But there was another sound that seemed to be between the other dogs and them. It was something big. The dogs were chasing it, and they were coming this way.

So they ran in the darkness. Emily and Sam ran ahead with the other dogs, and then they would take turns dropping back as if to check on their weaker human companions. Of these, Dianna ran ahead calling behind her what she knew of the path.

"This is where the path curves to the left with a slope! Just a few steps after that there is a big root that sticks out."

Paul ran behind the others and anticipated each of the obstacles as Dianna called them out. Every once in awhile he reached out to make sure Tony stepped over and around that which could have sent them falling. In a fleeting thought, Paul realized that Regina didn't seem to be having any trouble. In fact, she leaped over the branches and roots like a ballerina. Soon they reached the road. Dianna thought they were going to head into town to get help, but they didn't. The dogs kept running straight ahead. They ran across the road, through another field and down into more woods.

They ran and they ran in the moonlight, too frightened to know they were out of breath or that the muscles in their legs were beginning to cramp. It was difficult to see in these woods. They were thick and the light from the moon and the stars wasn't able to seep through the crowded branches. It was hard not to panic. They each focused on the pack of dogs ahead of them. The sounds of their paws were all around them. It was the sounds that helped them to know where they were going. The sounds of the paws were what was saving them from what was behind them. And it was getting closer. They could hear the howling of the other dogs and they could hear big branches breaking as the bad thing got closer. Still they each tried to focus on the running sounds of the dogs who were leading them. If they concentrated on these sounds, they would be able to run in the right direction.

The sounds from the pack behind them were getting closer and closer. Paul could almost feel the wind from the running dogs that were quickly gaining on them. He was fighting panic, fighting, fighting, fighting. *Focus on the dogs. Focus on running.* He couldn't believe how loud the dogs he was running with were. He was grateful though. If they hadn't been that loud, he wouldn't have been able to stay focused. He didn't know that his thoughts were shared by the others. All of the two-legged creatures were concentrating on the sound of the running padded feet. All of them were grateful for how the sound seemed to surround them and keep them focused.

Suddenly they ran out into a clearing. The moonlight reached down to embrace them. For a moment they were safe. They looked around and each of them let out a gasp, for they were surrounded by their four-legged friends. That was how they were able to hear them so they would know where to go. The dogs had

Wicked Dreams

surrounded them and ran with them to make sure they got to safety.

Dianna turned to Paul and saw blood on his arm. She reached to him to see if he was all right. He was reaching for her face at the same time. Both of them were bloodied from tree branches and vines that had whipped at them while they were running through the dark woods. Regina and Tony looked no better. Sam, Emily and the others looked in better shape, but they were panting heavily.

"What's that smell?" Dianna finally spoke.

"It smells like gas," Tony answered.

"And that evil thing... that bad smell from our dreams," Paul gasped.

"But we never smell that without the butterflies." Dianna said.

"Where are they?" Regina finally was able to say something.

"Arrrrhghhhhh They're here! Arrr...arrr...arrr. And now they're not!" a loud and hairy voice came form the edge of the woods. And then, in vile contrast to the grace of the moonlight, out stepped Larry. His appearance had greatly changed over the last few days. He was taller, wider and harrier and he smelled like death. His eyes seemed to glow and they had a crazy look beyond even what they had before.

Regina screamed and fainted. Tony caught her and held her, afraid to set her down because he knew they would need to run again. But before they could flee, Larry surprised them by lighting a match. In the flickering light of the small flame, his face appeared as an evil magician about to perform the trick to end all tricks.

"It's really quite simple. Arrrgh Arrrgh Arrgh. I just drop this little matchy into this little field which I have been marinating in gasoliny and then, poof, the butterflies are all gone. All gone."

"They are all gone," Dianna felt strangely courageous.

"That's what I said, bitch!" the evil thing snapped back.

"No. I mean, they are all gone. I don't see any butterflies."

"What..." and then Larry's jaws dropped as he saw that all of the butterflies were floating on the edge of the woods. Apparently he had found their favorite resting spot. But the butterflies had been smart enough to stay away from the smell of the gasoline. Perhaps some sort of genetic memory warned them that this was how whole populations were murdered.

Still Larry stood with the match. When the light grew dim, he lit another as if uncertain what to do next. But he didn't have a chance to make up his mind because the Goddess of the Moon intervened again. Suddenly those clouds that had been hiding for the last several hours all filled the sky. There was a clap of thunder and then the field was washed clean with the downpour that ensued. The hard rain caught Larry by surprise, which gave the dogs and the humans just barely enough time to run into the woods again. As soon as they got far enough into the woods where Larry wouldn't be able to see them, they stopped. For some reason, they knew they weren't to run too far from the field.

They waited quietly, almost a hundred wild dogs, two domestics and four humans. They waited in the darkness, afraid to make any sound. Mosquitoes picnicked happily on their faces, arms, and legs. No one dared to slap them off for fear of the sound it would make. They waited in the dark afraid to breathe. They waited in the dark afraid to think of that which was only a few yards away. They waited in the dark for the inevitable to happen. And then they waited no more.

Just as they started to panic wondering what to do next, the dogs began to move. They surrounded Regina, Tony, Dianna and Paul. In the darkness the foursome found themselves groping for the fur of their four-legged friends. And then, ever so quietly, they headed in a roundabout way back to the meadow that had just been washed clean by the night storm. When they got to the clearing again, Emily and Sam stood in front of Dianna and the rest, facing them as if to tell them that they should stay where they were. The rest of the dogs headed out into the clearing. It was too dark to see what they were doing. And they moved so quietly it was hard to tell exactly where they were.

And then the clouds gently moved through the sky as though they were a curtain opening. The moon and starlight burst through the night and lit the meadow as if it were a stage. And in a way it was a stage, with the final act of this version of good versus evil about to begin.

Dianna and the others looked around the meadow and then they realized what the dogs had planned. The beast called Larry was in the middle of the field and he was surrounded by about a hundred wild dogs, all standing silently, watching the evil form that stood before them. Larry was angry and swatting his arms around his head. Silvery wings danced in the moonlight, fluttering around Larry's head, driving him further into the madness into which he had been descending.

"Arrrgggh!" he yelled as he lit another match.

"It's no good!" Dianna yelled across the field. "The rain washed all the gasoline away."

"Arrrggghhhh. You don't know that! You don't know that!" and with that Larry threw the match down into the tall grass. But nothing happened. He tried to break through the ring of dogs to get to his prey, but they wouldn't let him through. They would growl and snap at him and the imprisoning circle would move with him keeping him a safe distance from Dianna and the others.

The game went on for what seemed like an eternity. Larry seemed to be losing some strength, but not the dogs. They held their ground and gave no sign that they would give in. Finally, Larry seemed to be growing weaker and he reached for the matches again.

Again Dianna called out that there was no fuel for the fire. The rain had dampened the tall grass and washed away the gasoline. "It's all gone, Larry."

And again Larry responded with, "Arrrggghhhh. You don't know that! You don't know that!" But this time, before he could drop it in the grass, one of the dogs broke from the ring and attacked Larry, ferociously biting him in the left leg. Blood dripped down the dog's jaw as he held his grip, jerking his head back and forth ripping muscle and tendon from bone. The match Larry had been holding was forgotten in the sudden burst of pain. It fell from his hand, dropping down onto his clothing.

Now, no one had had the time to notice that when the rains came, Larry had been enough on the edge

Wicked Dreams

of the woods that the tempest had not reached him. And Larry had been so fixed on that night's killing that he had failed to notice a good deal of the gasoline he had sprayed over the field had splattered onto his own clothing. All of these things happened unnoticed, but were suddenly understood as Larry burst into flames.

Larry screamed a horribly inhuman scream and ran. The others watched in horror as the fiery flames in the shape of a man escaped through the meadow and disappeared into the night. They stood still and silent as they looked into each other's eyes. They couldn't believe what had just happened, but the smell left behind was proof that their eyes had not deceived them.

Dianna, Paul, Regina and Tony began to walk back through the field, but the dogs remained rigid. Dianna turned to Emily and saw her friend standing next to Sam and they were both staring out across the meadow in the direction Larry had fled. The wild dogs were in the same pose.

"Do you guys really think it's over?" Dianna asked.

"No one could survive that," Paul answered wrapping his arm around Dianna's shoulders.

They all turned to watch the dogs who stood still and silent looking into the future.

"Still...."

"Oh, no!" Dianna was interrupted by Regina. "It's not! It's not over!"

They all turned to look at Regina and then their gazes dropped to what Regina held in her hand. And there in the moonlight, they saw the small wooden figure that Mr. Carver had made for her. And there in the moonlight they saw what had become a small wooden clone of Larry. And there in the moonlight they all realized that it was not over. For why would Maggie have made sure they knew of the powers of this weapon, if not to use it?

Before they could wonder what to do next, they saw a chain reaction fall across the dogs that surrounded them. In the low haunting song of howls that came next, there was another sound that was coming closer and closer. It was the sound of whooshing footsteps. It was the sound of breaking branches and crushing grass. And it was the sound of crackling fire. Suddenly, the flaming evil thing came rushing towards them. Amid the sound of snapping fire and the smell of burning hair was unmistakingly the sound of someone laughing. And as it burned and laughed, it came barreling after them. They ran for the woods and were just about there when Paul stumbled over a large rock that had been hidden in the tall grass. He tried to keep his balance, but wasn't able to. In slow motion he stumbled and stumbled, step after step, until he crashed to the ground. The others started to run back to help him when Tony yelled at Regina and Dianna to go on.

"Go! Get out of here!" Paul and Tony yelled at the other two.

But Regina and Dianna didn't really have a choice. Emily, Sam and the other dogs had surrounded them and were herding them back into the woods. When they reached the edge, Dianna turned around and let out a scream that could be heard above all of the other noises of panic. For when Dianna turned around she

Wicked Dreams

saw the evil thing that burned in the shape of a man was only a few feet away from Paul and Tony.

Paul was pushing Tony away from him, and Dianna could tell that he was trying to get Tony to leave him. And then Tony stopped. He stood up and turned to face what had once been Larry. He then turned to look at Regina who stood by Dianna's side at the edge of the woods. And just as Dianna thought Tony was going to honor Paul's demands, he spun around on his heels and ran towards the attacker. He got up good enough speed that when he reached the human fire, the impact knocked them both to the ground. Tony held tight to the beast not letting it go. He held and held and held as the two tumbled through the tall grass, rolling back and forth. But then his body finally gave in to the fire that consumed him. As Dianna saw Tony's body collapse she turned to Regina. But the look on Regina's face wasn't one of horror. It was the look that someone gets when they finally understand that which had been beguiling them. She held up her hand. And there in her palm rested the small wooden man.

Before Dianna could stop her, Regina bolted toward the fire that was again moving swiftly toward Paul. But she didn't run alone. She was encircled by four-legged beasts who shared her mission. She stopped when she reached a spot of ground that was between Paul and the thing. She stood still and held the wooden figure up as though it was a sword. The animals surrounded her, a circle of protection, a circle of good. The human fire came closer and then slowed as though confused by this turn of events. And then it seemed to understand. It moved as though it were going to attack Regina, but as soon as it got close

Amy J. Cooper

enough that she felt sure of success, Regina hurled the little wooden Larry at the fire. The explosion that ensued shook the earth for miles and miles. It forced the nearby tall and ancient trees to bend and burn. And it lit the night sky like a thunderous cloudburst of daylight.

About the Author

In 1992, Amy Cooper married her childhood sweetheart, Gregory, who is also a writer. They live in a cozy little ranch home on 3.5 acres surrounded by a stream in a rural area just south of beautiful Circleville, Ohio. As an adult learner, Amy earned her Bachelor of Arts degree from Capital University and her Master's Degree from Franklin University; both located in Columbus, Ohio. She enjoys spending time with her husband and their three adopted dogs, running, hiking, riding motorcycles, writing, reading and more. She has already begun work on her next project, so look for more from Amy J. Cooper!

Printed in the United States
27201LVS00001B/244-327